Emelio held utterly still in that watchful and predatory manner she'd come to know

But his eyes gave him away. Staring into the depths of his amber-green gaze, Stevie knew she had reached him on a primal level at last. Regret darkened his features a second before he stepped back.

"I have a strict policy against workplace relationships."

"We're nowhere near the P.I. agency now," she pointed out. Stevie leaned around him, making sure her breasts brushed across his arm.

"You still work for me, Stevie."

"No problem. I quit."

"Resignation duly noted," he said wryly. "But the policy is in place for a good reason. Sleeping with someone who works for you clouds your judgment."

"So who said anything about *sleep?*"

His nostrils flared and she saw his pupils dilate. She was standing close enough to hear the quick intake of breath before he shook his head. "Even if I accepted your resignation, which I don't, that doesn't solve anything. You asked me to take you on as a client. The same policy applies."

"Not a problem," she whispered, "you're fired."

Dear Reader,

Stevie Madison is smart, sexy and spirited. But even a tough girl has a tender side, as Emelio Sanchez soon discovers. She's been sending him erotic notes signed, "Yours in Black Lace." When the fiercely independent security expert goes on the run with the overprotective investigator, Emelio has to guard his heart against Stevie's seductive charms.

It takes a special kind of hero to be matched with a strong and determined woman. Some of you may remember Emelio from my last book. Those who are meeting him for the first time, prepare to fall in love. Emelio offers Stevie exactly the kind of affection and understanding she needs to heal the wounds of her past.

Everyone wishes for a happy ending, and certainly Stevie and Emelio's comes true. I wish you happy reading. I wish you joy. Please visit at www.miazachary.com.

Mia Zachary

Books by Mia Zachary

HARLEQUIN BLAZE

83—RED SHOES & A DIARY

YOURS IN BLACK LACE

Mia Zachary

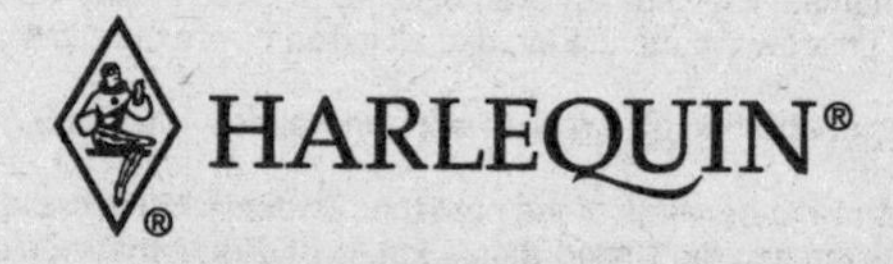

TORONTO • NEW YORK • LONDON
AMSTERDAM • PARIS • SYDNEY • HAMBURG
STOCKHOLM • ATHENS • TOKYO • MILAN • MADRID
PRAGUE • WARSAW • BUDAPEST • AUCKLAND

This one is for my Wonder Muffin, my hero for the past twelve years, and for my Precious Angel, a little hero in training. Love you, guys.

ACKNOWLEDGMENTS

The year 2003 was one of the most difficult years of my life, one full of loss and change. There's no way I could have finished this book without the help, support and red ink of my critique partners: Kelly, Lisa, Sheryl, Maryanne and Dee. I'm eternally grateful.

ISBN 0-373-79140-2

YOURS IN BLACK LACE

This edition published by arrangement with Harlequin Books S.A.

www.eHarlequin.com

Printed in U.S.A.

Black-Lace Letter Number One

You're all I think about, all that I dream of. I can't wait to get my hands on you. I want to strip you bare and pleasure your gorgeous body in the most erotic ways.

In my fantasy, I slowly unbutton your shirt and slip it off your shoulders. As I lightly stroke your neck and chest, I feel your skin heat beneath my fingers. Then my hands glide lower, over your belly and down to your waist.

I unsnap your jeans and slide the zipper down. Then I push them, along with your shorts, over your hips and down your thighs, leaving you naked at last.

I take my time, touching and tasting and enjoying you. I wait to hear you moan and whisper my name. Then, and only then, will I be…

Yours, in black lace.

1

HE WAS READING one of her letters. She recognized the pearl-gray note card right away. Stephanie Madison stood in the doorway of Emelio Sanchez's office and concentrated on him, instead of the packet she was gripping in her left hand.

South Florida sunlight poured through the large windows, flashed off the steel-and-smoked-glass desk, highlighting Emelio's coffee-brown hair. Tousled strands fell loosely around his face then were absently pushed aside, his attention focused on the provocative words she'd written for him.

Stevie took advantage of his distraction, using the time to study features she'd already committed to memory on her first day at January Investigations. It was a compelling face, a blend of cool reserve and masculine appeal too beautiful to be called handsome and yet devastatingly male.

Her eyes roamed over his strong jaw, regal nose and the high ridge of his cheekbones. His hazel eyes, she knew, were flecked with amber and green and the shadows of distant secrets. His lips were firm and full in a wide mouth that rarely smiled.

Just now, there was a slight softening of his normally brooding features. Had the contents of her letter gotten to him? She hoped so. Dreams about Emelio, about what she wanted to do with him, made for long, frustrating nights. Her pulse accelerated and a delicious longing settled into her belly.

She'd been lusting after her boss ever since she joined the agency. But only on paper. Women called the office for him all the time, so she didn't stand much of a chance with a playboy who was already juggling at least three girlfriends. Still, she hadn't been able to resist the urge to write down her fantasies.

There was power and magic in words, because once she dared to put her thoughts on paper, she started to give Emelio the occasional flirtatious glance or inviting smile at work. When the looks he sent her in return began to hold a bit more than professional interest, she took a chance and mailed him one of her letters. Over the past four months, she'd sent eight more.

But she hadn't yet figured out when or how to tell him of her attraction. Somehow the timing never seemed right. And, truthfully, she liked controlling the situation for now. She wanted to seduce his mind before she risked going after his body. She'd changed a lot, was almost a completely different person than the girl who'd fled New Orleans five years ago. However, inside, the fear of rejection, of not being good enough, remained.

Stevie continued to admire the sight of him. How could any man look so good in a polo shirt the color of pistachio ice cream? The pastel green material offset the golden brown of his skin and emphasized his muscular shoulders and broad chest. The short sleeves wrapped snugly around rock-solid biceps. But Emelio's hands fascinated her most.

Long, tapered fingers curved around the letter he

held. His hands had a surprising eloquence that accompanied his words when he spoke. Those hands had haunted her for months now. She longed to feel them cradle her neck as he kissed her, then slide along her bare skin until his fingers delved lower, making her moan with pleasure.

She must have made some sound because his head came up fast, like a wolf sensing danger. His amber-green eyes shimmered with a sensual heat before the emotion vanished behind his professional mask. In the same instant, he turned the letter facedown on his desk and brought his left hand out of his lap.

Stevie assumed her words had caused his need for adjustment but suppressed a grin. She wished she could give in to the laughter but for one thing, Emelio had no idea she'd been mailing him the erotic notes. For another, she was too damn upset to laugh right now.

All last night, she'd lain in bed awake, startling at the slightest noise, fighting the restless urge to escape into a glass of wine. As a result, her skin felt too tight, as if all of her nerve endings were exposed. She clutched the envelope in front of her as she stepped onto the gray-and-black area rug.

"Did I disturb you, Emelio?"

He cleared his throat, but a trace of huskiness remained. "No. Come on in."

Out of habit, she looked over at the original José Castillo paintings on the wall as she passed by. The bold slashes of color swirling across the canvases seemed out of place in the stylishly austere corner office.

"You always do that."

Stevie shifted her gaze at the sound of his voice.

"I know. It's impossible to look away. The artist's work is so...passionate."

Passion. Lately the only passion he experienced was vicarious, through either art or words. Emelio leaned back in his leather executive chair and glanced down at the latest note from his secret seductress. Just as with the last seven letters, these erotic images burned themselves into his brain.

> *Your fingertips graze the fabric of my black panties, tickling the tender skin along my inner thigh. Reaching under the lace edge, you feel my damp heat. I'm slick with need and gasping with pleasure as your fingers slide inside...*

It had been a while, but his body remembered. Anticipation heated his skin and an aching erection throbbed against his zipper. The anonymous notes intrigued him, but he still had no idea who his imaginary lover was.

"Can you make time for a new client?"

Emelio pushed the *black-lace letter* from his thoughts and sat forward, resting his arms on the edge of the desk.

"Of course. Who is it?"

"Me."

Stevie settled into the guest chair, crossing her endless legs at the knee, and shoved the sleeves of her thin cotton sweater past her elbows.

He looked at her, really looked, for the first time since she'd walked in. Beneath a layered cap of hair every shade from honey to sand, her normally vivid complexion seemed pale against the turquoise-blue sweater. Otherwise, she was as striking as ever. Her skin was flawless and he imagined it felt as soft as a child's. Her face was beautiful, despite an old break that marred the straight line of her nose. Her bottom lip was broader than the top, giving her a sensual pout.

Stevie's mouth always looked ready to be kissed. And that was one temptation he couldn't allow himself. The fact that she worked for him put her strictly off-limits. He'd once learned a deadly lesson about mixing business with pleasure, a lesson he would never forget.

The delicacy of Stevie's features belied the enigmatic strength evident in her direct, almost aggressive, gaze. The color of her gray-blue eyes shifted like clouds across a summer sky. "Tiffnee signed for this yesterday before she shut down the phones for the night."

Her watch, a man's Timex that was too big for her slender wrist, clinked against the desk as she slid a packet across the surface. The plain manila envelope bore no address or postmark. "Madison" was written with black marker in letters uniform enough to have been stenciled onto the paper.

Disquiet slithered over him as he turned the envelope over and carefully removed the contents. Emelio stared at the glossy four-by-six photos. Surveillance photos of Stevie.

"Do you have any idea who sent these, or why?"

Her lush mouth twisted into a frown. "Believe me, I've been racking my brain all night. I thought it might be backlash from some case I'd investigated. Oh, wait, I forgot. I haven't done any fieldwork yet."

Emelio ignored the edge in her voice. "You were hired because we needed a security specialist."

"Okay, well, I've spent ten months installing alarm systems and pulling guard duty for movie sets and society parties. Now I'm ready for an undercover assignment."

He remembered some of the assignments from his days with the FBI. Undercover work wasn't as glamorous as Hollywood made it seem. It was tense and tiring, lonely and frustrating. He looked at Stevie's fresh, eager face and shook his head. "You're not ready."

He returned his attention to the first photograph. She wore a formfitting tank top and spandex shorts. She should wear spandex more often because the pliant material showed off one of the finest backsides he'd ever seen. Emelio forced himself to study the street, the pedestrians and the environment, searching for clues to the stalker's identity.

"Tell me if you recognize anyone."

"I was going into my gym. I know the women walking behind me. They're regulars in my kickboxing class, but those pictures could have been taken almost any Tuesday night."

He glanced up at her. "Kickboxing."

She gave a sassy little shrug. "It's part of my training program, along with Tai Bo and weight lifting. I want to be ready when you finally let me do real work."

He rolled his eyes and looked at the next picture.

"Those were taken outside the grocery store. Judging by the outfit I had on, I'm guessing it was last Monday. But this—" she tapped a blunt nail against the next photo and her indignation almost succeeded in masking the catch in her voice "—this shows me leaving the bank and that was goddamn yesterday."

He examined the last picture. *Mierda!* Emelio inhaled sharply and a hot rush of surprise and anger clawed at his chest. Barely visible in the corner of the photograph, he immediately recognized a man with salt-and-pepper hair and deceptively cultured features.

Rogelio Braga. The one who had got away.

Before starting January Investigations with Alex Worth, his partner and best friend, Emelio had worked for the Justice Department in the Special Operations Division. Braga liked to play the part of a quiet, respectable businessman, but he was in fact a money launderer and second in command of a notorious drug-trafficking cartel.

Emelio's first undercover assignment for the SOD was to find proof that the Dominican cartel was moving drugs and cash through a Miami travel agency. The investigation had gone south when his informant betrayed him. His cover got blown, Alex was wounded and the informant had been killed. He shouldered his responsibility for the screwup and for the death, but it really burned him that Braga had skated on all charges.

"Do you recognize anybody in this one?" He forced the words past the cold rage threatening to choke him.

"Maybe." Stevie cocked her head to the side to get a better look. She pointed to Braga. "I never forget a face, and I know I've seen his before, but I can't place him."

"There must be something. Think, Stevie." He held the picture out to her, wanting to jar her memory.

She pushed it away. "Don't you think I have been? Just because there's no menacing note with those photos, doesn't mean I don't feel violated and threatened. Some creep is following me around, watching me..."

She squared her shoulders and gave him a challenging stare. "The question is, how do I handle it? I want to set up some kind of countersurveillance—"

"I think you should disappear."

Her straight, golden eyebrows arched toward her hairline. "Excuse me?"

He slid the pictures back inside the envelope, handling them carefully by the edges. While his actions were slow and methodical, his mind raced with possibilities. Braga was sending a message, but damned if he knew exactly why, or how Stevie could be involved. He had to get her out of danger's way until he could figure out what Braga was after.

"Whoever is stalking you may be a shy admirer, but more likely they mean you real harm." Emelio glanced at the thin gold watch on his wrist. "You've got twenty minutes to wrap up whatever files are on your desk. Is there someplace you can stay?"

She shot to her feet. "Wait a minute. I'm a professional in an agency full of other professionals. I'll admit to being a little freaked out, but there's no reason—"

"Nineteen minutes and forty seconds, Stevie. Come get me when you're ready to leave and I'll drive you wherever you want to go."

She crossed her arms defiantly, enhancing her cleavage as the cotton material stretched across her breasts. Her round, full, perfectly shaped breasts. Emelio dropped his gaze but found himself eyeing her slim hips and sleekly muscled thighs instead.

"I'm not running again."

"Again?" He looked up.

Her eyes darted away, then back. Her tone had revealed more than she'd intended. "I did my best secret-agent impression to get a cab here this morning. It looks more fun in the movies."

"Then don't think of it as running. It's a strategic retreat." The telephone rang before she could retort. "Yes? Put her through, Tiffnee, thank you." Emelio cupped one hand over the receiver. "Seventeen minutes, fifty. Go."

This was unbelievable. She still wasn't being allowed to do fieldwork, not even on her own case! She felt her temper shift from *annoyed* into *irate*. Another good-looking, arrogant, overbearing male thought he could control her life.

"*Hola,* Connie. How are you?" He shot a pointed glance at the door in a bid for privacy.

And *infuriated* was on the horizon. Emelio had just blatantly dismissed her to take a call from one of his girlfriends, and she wasn't going to stand for it. After giving him a nasty look, she flopped back down on the guest chair.

Emelio sighed and began to speak in Spanish. Stevie gave him the courtesy of turning her head, but she couldn't shut her ears. His voice was affectionate and warm, and, though she didn't understand what he said, his tone held an underlying tenderness that cut straight to her heart. She felt jealous, embarrassed at eavesdropping on his intimate conversation, but she wasn't going anywhere, damn it.

Finally, he said, "Okay, *cariña.* I'll call you later, I promise."

She snapped at him before he'd even hung up the

phone. "You know more than you're saying, Emelio. Since this involves me, tell me what's going on."

He held her gaze, searching for something, obviously debating how much to reveal. Then he set his features and lied to her, she'd swear to it.

"I don't know anything, Stevie. I only suspect. So, you're taking a leave of absence from work until I can get to the bottom of this."

"I'm not some damsel in distress that needs a big strong guy to keep me out of trouble. It's my life that may be in danger—"

"Trust me. You are in danger."

She cocked her head to one side, baiting him. "But you just said you don't know for sure. So let me do what I've trained for. I'm nobody's victim, Emelio."

Not anymore, Stevie thought. *Never again.*

THE MADISON WOMAN had seen far too much and she could not be allowed to talk. She could ruin everything he'd worked toward. She had to be silenced.

Rogelio Braga studied the photograph on the table before him, brushing his fingers lightly over the slick surface. She was quite lovely, despite her short hair and masculine name. What made her most attractive was her usefulness as an instrument of revenge.

His gaze shifted to the man beside her in the picture, the man he planned to destroy. Emelio Sanchez had made the grave error of allowing his feelings to show and the camera had recorded the moment. Falling in love would be the death of him; Braga would make sure of it.

He lit a cigarette and imagined another face, another time. Braga crushed the photograph in his fist.

Yes, Sanchez would pay. First with the Madison woman's life and then with his own.

THEY'D SPENT THE LAST ten of her twenty minutes in heated debate.

"I don't see why you're being so unreasonable. If it were Jason or one of the other guys, you'd be all for it."

"Fine, I admit it. I'm an old-fashioned guy with a protective streak toward the fairer gender. But my decision is based on level of experience—"

"This is the twenty-first century, Emelio. A woman can do just about anything a man can. She doesn't need to hide behind him. I don't need to hide."

He came around the desk and loomed over her, as if trying to use his size and stubbornness to intimidate her. "You know what I'm suggesting is the most logical solution. If you want to be treated like a professional, then act like one."

His attitude was all it took for her to hit seriously pissed off. Stevie got in Emelio's face, her height and two-inch heels putting her almost at his eye level. Stevie tried to concentrate on her argument, but the citrus and spice aftershave Emelio wore kept distracting her. She could feel the warmth emanating from his incredible body and the dark wisps of chest hair visible in the opening of his shirt was turning her on.

It didn't matter that he was a walking pheromone, though. He was still a domineering dictator seriously jeopardizing her chance for career advancement. Her therapist would be proud that she'd, one, identified her emotions and, two, focused on the source. She was just about to follow step three, voicing her feelings, when the receptionist walked in.

"Jeez, Emelio, you got, like, a ton of mail today." Tiffnee bounced over to where they stood glaring at each other, oblivious to the tension in the air.

He finally broke Stevie's stare to acknowledge the bundle of mail thrust at him with a brief nod. "Thanks, Tiffnee."

"No problem, boss." The perky brunette grinned at him, revealing a wad of bright pink bubblegum. "Hey, Stevie. Great sweater. Beau-tique, right? I saw it last time I went shopping at Aventura Mall."

She was irritated by the interruption, but being nasty to Tiffnee was a sin on par with kicking a puppy. So she listened as the girl launched into an inane conversation about the latest fashions. Out of the corner of her eye, Stevie recognized a small pearl-gray envelope. She saw Emelio tuck her ninth erotic note in his back pocket and continue to sort through the mail.

"Tiffnee."

The receptionist turned her head in the same instant Stevie did, both of them alerted to the tone of his voice. In the space of a heartbeat Stevie realized that Emelio held a plain manila packet in his hand.

"Oh, yeah. I forgot to tell you." Tiffnee pursed her rosebud lips in apology. "The messenger who just left said that one was, like, urgent."

Emelio dropped the mail and sprinted for the door.

"Urgent means right-away-immediately-now, Tiff." Stevie bent over and snatched the packet off the floor. "Sanchez" was written in thick black marker, just like on the envelope she got. She ripped it open with fingers gone cold from dread. A precisely cut article from the *Miami Herald* lay on top of another stack of photographs.

DRUG CZAR TRIAL CONTINUES

After a series of legal delays, Francisco Guillermo Ramos, who was arrested last year at a Florida Keys resort on several counts of drug trafficking and money laundering, is scheduled to take the stand…

Tiffnee leaned in close to read over her shoulder. "Hey, that's the trial Em and Alex testified at a few weeks ago."

Stevie made a sound of acknowledgement before flipping the newsprint under the photos. She blinked in confusion. Who the hell had taken these? The pictures showed her in a guard uniform, arms stretched wide to hold back a crowd of onlookers.

"I remember that. Miramax asked us to provide extra security while they were filming *Angelfire* near the Bayside Marketplace."

Tiffnee grabbed her arm. "Ooh, I just love Will Smith! He's so hot."

The next photo was of Emelio standing watch outside of a large white trailer, then one of them together near the expensive car used in the movie's chase scenes. Stevie shuffled the stack to the last picture and the breath caught in her throat. She stared at the close-angle shot.

Her head was turned to the left, smiling at something out of view. Emelio stood beside her and the camera had captured his unguarded expression. Several indefinable emotions were reflected in his gaze, lighting his hazel eyes with a smoldering intensity.

"Wow, Stevie. That man wants you bad."

She choked out a laugh. If she wasn't looking at Mr. Calm, Cool and Controlled with her own eyes, she never would have believed the depth of his regard. A warm tingling feeling spread through her body and settled in the apex of her thighs. *That man wanted her bad.*

Just then Emelio came back into his office. Tiffnee snatched the one picture and shoved it inside her T-shirt. She whispered under her breath, "I'll put this in your purse."

Stevie turned to Emelio, hoping her expression showed concern and not unexpected delight. His dark hair was swept back from his forehead as if he'd shoved it out of his eyes, revealing the small stud in his left ear and giving him a fresh-from-bed sexiness. "Did you find him?"

He scowled and stalked across the room, moving with his signature long, fluid stride. "I took the stairs since the elevators are notoriously slow, but I didn't see any messenger."

Stevie listened closely while Tiffnee briefly described the "blond hottie" who'd delivered both packages.

"I want a full, written description of him, everything he said and anything else you remember."

"For sure, boss. Like, written written or typed written?" At the look he gave her, the receptionist backed toward the door. "Never mind. I'll figure it out."

Emelio shook his head as she bounced back out the door. "That girl is lucky she's Alex's cousin."

Stevie passed him the contents of the manila envelope. "I'd say this blows your 'harmless admirer' theory."

"Feel free to open my mail."

"I did, thanks."

Emelio sank into his chair while reading the article,

his brooding expression firmly in place. Considering he'd just run down ten flights, there was only the faintest sheen of sweat on his forehead and he wasn't even out of breath. A woman had to admire that kind of stamina.

She sauntered around the desk and rested one hip on the edge, allowing her blue-and-white skirt to creep up her thigh an inch or so. "That headline relates to your investigation at the Cayo Sueño Resort, right?"

Against his better judgment, Emelio allowed his gaze to travel. It moved from the long, slim thigh, over her knee and along her shapely calf to the high-heeled sandal dangling off her bare toes. It took him a second to remember her question. He raised his focus to Stevie's face.

"Yeah, we were working an SOD case against the Dominican cartel. Alex went undercover down in the Keys as an investment broker, trying to use a man named Rogelio Braga to get to Frankie Ramos, former head of the cartel. I operated behind the scenes to gather evidence of money laundering. Braga disappeared two days before the arrest, but we finally took down Ramos and seized over a hundred million dollars from their organization."

"I didn't work on that case. So I don't understand what this has to do with me." She indicated the pictures from the movie set.

"Neither do I. Not yet."

As he laid the newest set of photos on the desktop, he accepted that Stevie's safety was now his responsibility. He didn't want to tell her any more than necessary, not until he was sure. But it seemed obvious Braga intended to use Stevie to get to him. Braga prided himself on being a man who never forgot a favor. Or a slight.

Emelio had more than slighted him. He had infiltrated the cartel right under the man's nose. *Gracias a Dios,* Alex had taken his wife, Meghan, and their newborn son to Baltimore to visit her family. That was three less people he had to worry about.

"I want to be on the road within the next hour."

Stevie's eyes darkened to a stormy gray, her sexy pout twisting into a frown. "Where are *you* going?"

"Wherever you go, lady. I'm not leaving your side."

A warm frisson of awareness passed between them. Her pupils dilated in the dark blue depth of her gaze and he heard the quick intake of breath before she turned her normally subtle Southern accent into a sensual drawl.

"I don't need a bodyguard, Emelio. I am a bodyguard. Well, at least I've been through the training."

"Then you know how it works. We stay together 24/7 until this is over."

2

STEVIE FORCED ASIDE all thought of danger until she focused on getting Emelio alone. She was going to have him to herself, twenty-four hours a day...and night. That was definitely the silver lining in the dark cloud hanging over her life right now.

A spark of excitement ignited in her belly. She'd spent the past four months creating the seduction. Now she was going to climb over the professional wall standing between them and, with any luck, land right in his lap. With a little planning, and a lot of opportunity, she could move their work relationship to an up-close-and-personal level.

The photograph that had captured his rare moment of openness was hidden in her handbag, but she didn't need to take it out to remember Emelio's expression. That look of unguarded lust had her feeling hot and tingly. So did the touch of his hand on her forearm.

Emelio stood in front of her, checking in all directions as he held the freight elevator open. His palm felt smooth and warm and strong and a bolt of desire shot though her. How many nights had she dreamed of having his hands stroke and caress her? How many times had she settled for her own?

Excitement hummed along her veins as her eyes roamed over him. His long hair touched the top of his collar in dark waves. The pistachio cotton shirt stretched across the wide expanse of his back was tucked into a pair of black jeans that molded to his butt and thighs.

The guy looked just as good going as coming.

A grin spread over her face. She hadn't seen him coming yet. But she hoped to before the week was out. Stevie sobered her expression just as Emelio turned his head and nodded.

"All clear."

His hand slid down to clasp her fingers, and the casual touch sent ripples of longing throughout her body. After another glance around, he led her down the cement-block hallway toward the service entrance. She stumbled as she followed him across the alleyway to the parking garage.

"Slow down, will you? I'm wearing sandals." He shortened his stride with an apology, allowing her to catch up. To her surprise, he bypassed the VIP slots at the front of the garage. "Isn't that your Lexus parked right over there?"

"Yeah, it is. We're taking another car."

Her hand flexed involuntarily beneath his when her pulse leaped with a different kind of excitement. "What are you going to do, hot-wire one?"

"Something like that."

He looked around once more and let go of her hand before opening the door to the stairwell. She felt an odd sense of separation at the loss of contact. She also felt her calves screaming in protest.

"You take the stairs. These shoes are more decorative than functional. I'm catching the elevator."

"One, we don't want to get trapped in an elevator if anyone's waiting for us. And two, we're only going up two flights. You'll live."

Her sandals clattered on the concrete. ''My life has become a spy-thriller movie.''

''Oh, yeah? Which Bond girl are you?'' When he glanced at her a flash of amusement lit his hazel eyes.

''I always thought Holly Goodhead was a great name.'' She smirked when his step faltered. The flare of heat in his eyes was quickly extinguished, but she saw it. And she would use it to her advantage later. ''But I'd rather be Wai Lin, the heroine in *Tomorrow Never Dies.*''

''You don't look Chinese.''

''Funny. She was the best, very strong and independent. Her character was more Bond's equal. You should watch that film before assigning the next interesting case to one of the guys.''

''I like Sean Connery's Bond girls better. You can't go wrong with a woman named Pussy Galore.''

Stevie wrinkled her forehead and grimaced. ''I don't even know how to respond to that.''

''How about, 'Ooh, James'?''

A chuckle escaped her at his impression of the line spoken by every woman in every Bond movie. Great body, bad-boy attitude and a sense of humor. What more could she ask for?

As Emelio pushed open the level-three entrance, Stevie took a quick look around and then followed him toward the corner parking spaces. It was all very stealthy and exciting. She watched him walk to the passenger side of a silver sports car and pretend to check the tires. Then he reached inside the wheel well and pulled out a small metal box. Inside was a set of keys.

''Well, I'm disappointed. I thought I was finally going to learn how to hot-wire.''

"I'll teach you some other time." He unlocked the passenger door and held it open for her.

She lowered herself onto the gray leather seat and swung her legs inside. "Mmm. Very nice. Whose car is this?"

"It's registered to the corporation, so technically it belongs to the agency." He shut her in and walked around the rear of the vehicle.

By the time he reached the other side, she was already in the driver's seat. She rolled down the window when he tapped impatiently on the glass. "Since it's the agency's car, I get to drive. Hop in, handsome, and I'll take you for a ride."

At her choice of words frown lines appeared between his eyebrows, warring with a flash of sexual interest in his gaze. Then his expression cleared and she saw the corner of his mouth relax, though it wasn't quite a smile.

Emelio nodded once in agreement. "Makes sense, since you know the way to your apartment."

She started the engine and snuggled into the driver's seat. "Sweet getaway car. Does it have a rocket launcher or remote-controlled steering?"

"You watch way too many movies." He handed her the card key to get past the garage's electronic gate.

As she turned her head to check for oncoming traffic, a beige sedan idling against the curb caught her eye. Looking at the man behind the wheel triggered alarms in her brain. "Emelio, I think that's the messenger Tiffnee described."

He swung his head to where she indicated. "Start driving and see if he follows."

She eased out into traffic, trying to watch where

she was going and peer into the rearview mirror at the same time. The presence of the messenger was unnerving, but she welcomed the challenge. She'd always wanted to drive a getaway car.

Emelio's cell phone began to chime. "Hello? Angie. I can't— Yes, I know—"

Didn't those women ever stop calling him? The sudden stab of jealousy annoyed the hell out of her, but she didn't have time to dwell on it. "The beige sedan is pulling away from the curb, heading this way."

"We'll have to talk later, *cariña.*" He disconnected the call and tossed the phone into the beverage holder.

Cariña, again. He could at least show enough imagination to give his girlfriends different endearments. Envy had her growling as she glanced in the mirror again. "He's only two cars behind us now."

"Find someplace to pull over."

"Forget it. We'll be perfect targets." Stevie waited until the traffic light turned yellow. Then she shifted down into second gear and hit the gas. The powerful V-6 engine roared in response and she peeled across the intersection, tires squealing.

"Are you crazy?" Emelio braced one arm against the door handle and tightened his seat belt. He held his breath until they shot past the delivery van barreling toward his side of the car. "What the hell do you think you're doing?"

Staring straight ahead, Stevie answered him through gritted teeth. "I'm trying to lose the bad guy."

He rolled his eyes, unsure whether to laugh or pray. But a glance in the side-view mirror confirmed that the beige sedan had dodged the car in front of it and run the red light. *Mierda!* Thanks to Braga, and the wild woman beside him, he was going to end up a big smear on the pavement.

He turned his head to look at Stevie in case she was the last thing he ever saw. Her color was high and a daredevil grin split her face as she gripped the steering wheel in both hands and sped around a motorcycle. She was really loving this. And he was going to die.

"Hang a right onto First Street, then we'll switch places so that I can drive."

Stevie cut across to the far lane, downshifted and took the turn on two wheels. "I'm an expert at this, Emelio. I've been trained in high-speed, evasive and counterambush driving techniques."

"Counter. Ambush. You're kidding, right?" When he snickered, she shot him an offended glance.

She darted in and out between slower-moving cars. "No. I took a couple of classes with a former Secret Service agent. Graduated with honors, too."

Of course she had. Out of nowhere, he wondered if she approached sex the same way. Just the thought of being on the receiving end of all that relentless enthusiasm got him hard. What the hell was going on? He'd never considered sleeping with her before. And he couldn't consider it now.

Emelio checked the mirror again. "Damn, that beige sedan won't let up."

"No problem." She slowed the car, as if stopping for another light, then whipped the steering wheel to the left and raced along East Flagler Street. "I'm serious about doing fieldwork, Emelio. I'm ready."

"Can we talk about this later?" He closed his eyes

and waited for the impact when she tried to pass the freight truck in front of them.

"I've studied martial arts, explosives recognition, tactical firearms and hostage survival skills."

"We're private investigators, Stevie, not the Navy SEALs."

"Just know, I'm not giving up on this. I'm tired of sitting behind a desk designing alarm systems."

"Later." His heart leaped into his throat as she made a hard right around a minivan and careened onto Second Avenue.

"Listen, I'm more than qualified for the job—"

"Watch out!" He had to yell over the blare of honking horns. "Didn't any of those classes teach you how to read a One Way sign?"

She managed to evade the oncoming cars and got off on Fourth Street. From behind them, Emelio heard the squeal of brakes followed by the crunch of metal against metal. He looked back to confirm the beige sedan was no longer behind them.

"Hoo yah!"

He turned at Stevie's victory shout, not surprised to see her triumphant grin. Her cheeks were flushed, her blue eyes alive with excitement, and he imagined she'd wear that same expression after a few hours in bed. Looking at her, he wasn't sure if the rush he felt was adrenaline or attraction. Either way he wanted to reach over and kiss her, long and hard.

Stevie finally slowed down to the posted speed limit, but his heart beat an unsteady tattoo and his right hand still had a death grip on the door handle. He ought to flay her alive for taking ten years off his life, then have her committed to the nearest asylum.

Instead, he answered her proud grin with a quirk of his eyebrow. "So. What other classes have you taken?"

THE DOOR WASN'T LOCKED.

Stevie stared at the entry to her apartment in numb confusion. Why wasn't the door closed all the way? She was sure she'd yanked it shut this morning—the door always stuck and that was the only way to get the lock to engage.

"Stay here."

Emelio nudged her aside and reached out to gently push the door wider. It swayed open enough to let him slip through. She watched him crouch down before moving along the hall to check the other rooms.

Stevie followed as far as the living room, then jerked to a sickened halt. Everything she owned was strewn across the floor.

The love seat and chairs had been upended; the cushions slashed open to spill fluffy white filling onto the carpet. Her framed prints had been knocked from the walls. Sunlight from the now bare windows reflected off the plastic CD cases scattered about, and her collection of romantic suspense novels and mysteries had been swept off the shelves.

Her gaze slowly traveled over the mess to see that the dining table was on its side and all of the glassware in the kitchen lay in shards on the ceramic tile. She didn't want to see what the bedroom and office looked like. Her hands clenched into fists even as she started to tremble. Comprehension, cold and piercing, crept along her veins until her body was frozen in place.

Someone had been here. Some unknown menace, some malicious stranger, had been inside her home.

The significance weighed on her heart and sank into the pit of her stomach like a rock. She'd come so far, only to find herself cornered again.

Well, some people fought when cornered, and these days she was one of them. Red-hot fury melted the tendrils of fear that gripped her throat, spurring her into action. Stevie dropped to the floor and started gathering her books, stacking them in neat piles beside her.

Her independence and self-confidence were so hard-won, and at such a great price, she wouldn't let a little thing like a break-in get to her. No way.

"I'm sorry, Stevie, but we have to go."

Emelio carefully set a broken picture frame against what was left of her glass coffee table. She ignored him and began arranging her music discs. While separating the club music from the classical, she worked on identifying her emotions.

Frustrated. She'd have to replace all of her glasses and dishes, things she'd proudly chosen for her first apartment. *Annoyed.* She hated housework at the best of times, but this callous destruction went way beyond her normal sloppiness. *Afraid...* Her heart beat erratically, causing fine tremors that shook her hands. She'd deal with that one later. It was safer to be angry.

"Leave that, will you? I don't know how long ago this happened. And I don't know if they'll be back."

"I'm cleaning up, Emelio. You can help by picking up the TV set and putting it back in the entertainment center."

"Just leave it! We've got to get out of here. Now." Emelio snatched the music from her hands and tossed it aside.

She looked up, a protest on the tip of her tongue until he grabbed her left arm, pulling her to her feet. The instinctive part of her brain took over. He was big, he was strong, he was male. And he'd just put his hands on her.

Stevie swung at him, landing a hard blow to his shoulder. He dropped her arm in surprise and raised both of his in front of him. She watched his hands come up, and her mind emptied of all thoughts but one—fight back.

In a flood of emotion, she experienced the same fear and humiliation and self-loathing she'd felt the last time a man had grabbed her. He'd dislocated her shoulder that time. She'd had to suffer not only the pain but also the uncertain sympathy of the emergency room intern who treated her.

She lashed out again and again, barely able to see through the red haze clouding her eyes. Her head was spinning with memories. She heard a grunt of pain when her knee connected with his thigh, heard the low growl issuing from her own throat, but she felt nothing....

She felt nothing?

Stevie slowly returned to the present. It was Emelio, not Tom. And he wasn't attacking her. He was trying to block her punches. In a split second, he captured both of her hands to keep her from harming either one of them anymore. Stevie took comfort from his warmth and the gentle way he held her fingers, but she couldn't meet his eyes.

God, what must he think of her? Her gaze locked on to the dark purple bruise developing over his chin. She'd done that.

On the one hand, she should be proud that she

hadn't hesitated to use her training. But on the other, she'd lost control and descended into violence. The realization that she hadn't escaped her past after all brought tears to her eyes.

"I'm sorry, Emelio. I... I'm sorry."

He blew out a long breath and she felt the tension leave him. "Was he the same guy who broke your nose?"

She twisted out of his grasp, shame bringing hot color to her cheeks. "I think the slight bend gives my nose character." Her attempt to lighten the mood fell flat when her voice cracked.

"Tell me about him." Emelio's gaze was soft, understanding, however, his voice was firm. She shook her head, but he gently persisted. "Is there any possibility he did this? I need to know what we're dealing with."

"Tom didn't trash my apartment. I made sure when I left New Orleans that nobody knew where I was going."

"Could your family have—?"

"The last people I'd ever tell are my family." Stevie turned to open the French doors.

He followed her outside to the balcony. "What happened, Stevie?"

"I guess I owe you an explanation, don't I?" She gave a short laugh of embarrassment and leaned one hip against the railing, her arms wrapped protectively over her waist. "There's not much to tell. I married young. I married wrong."

She stared blindly across the street at the Miami-Dade Community College campus. "It started off with Tom picking my clothes, suggesting what I should do, where I should go. It was important for the wife of an aspiring politician to project a certain image. Then things changed and he started to dictate every aspect of my life."

All of it was for her own good, of course. She wasn't capable of taking care of herself, wasn't smart enough to make her own decisions. And if she dared to ignore his advice... She shivered, remembering as if it were yesterday.

"Did you tell anyone? Try to get help?" Emelio's face had darkened with anger but his voice remained low, soothing and, most importantly, nonjudgmental. A few of the tears blurring her vision spilled over her lashes.

"My parents didn't believe a 'nice boy like Tom' would treat me that way. He just had 'a quick temper' and the best thing I could do was to keep him happy. Later, I tried to tell my brother, Eric, but he didn't believe me, either. That sort of thing doesn't happen to 'people like us.'"

His hazel eyes reflected his understanding as he brushed the tears from her face with the pad of his thumb. "You didn't call the police?"

"I was ashamed, Emelio. I felt trapped and alone and I thought if my own family didn't believe me, no one else would, either. Tom belittled me until I had no self-esteem left. He made me a prisoner in my own life. And I let him do it...."

"You were victimized, Stevie. You didn't do anything to deserve that. No woman ever deserves that."

Following his instincts, Emelio tried to gather her into his arms, wanting to offer the sympathy and compassion he knew she'd never accept from his words. She hesitated, tensing when he refused to acknowledge her body language and held on to her anyway.

Slowly, in resistant increments, she eased into his embrace. Her breathing became audible and then she cried, aching sobs that seemed torn from her soul.

Rocking gently from side to side, he tightened his grip as her tears soaked into his shirt. Pressing his mouth to her temple in a gesture of comfort, he stroked one hand over the corn-silk strands of her hair. He'd been denying his attraction to her, knowing it wasn't to be. But for the first time, he saw the vulnerable woman beneath her tough exterior, and it touched his heart in a way he couldn't allow.

Stevie's breath hitched and her crying subsided almost as quickly as it had begun. He swallowed the lump in his throat and tried to ignore the feel of her lean, athletic body against his. He wouldn't think about the way her soft, full breasts flattened against his chest or her long legs pressed between his thighs.

It would be a huge mistake to kiss her. But it had been so long since he'd allowed any contact with a woman that his body responded instinctively. Shameless desire filled him, lengthened and thickened him. Before the possibility fully formed in his mind, Stevie tilted her head back and brushed her mouth over the tender bruise on his chin. His heart thudded in his chest and a searing urgency rushed though him. Then she turned her face until their lips met.

He leaned forward, trying not to think about what a mistake this was. It was easier than he expected because his mind focused on discovering that her sexy pout tasted as delicious as he'd imagined. The kiss was soft, gentle and slow, but an underlying expectancy was building between them.

Stevie's mouth relaxed and parted beneath his, both inviting and daring him to deepen the kiss. Her skirt made a swishing sound as her hips swayed across his arousal. Her hands fisted in the material of his shirt, urging him closer. He wanted her, but he wouldn't compound what was already a serious lack of judgment. No man with any honor would take advantage of a woman in an emotionally fragile state.

Emelio reluctantly broke the kiss. He had a responsibility, a duty to keep her safe from Braga. Getting involved with Stevie would only increase the danger to them both. He gently placed one hand on her shoulder and took a step back, putting some distance between them.

Stevie's full lips looked even more lush when thoroughly kissed and damned if he didn't want to do it again. Her cheeks bloomed with color and her eyes had taken on a somnolent expression. He kept his gaze from straying to the rapid rise and fall of her chest and the hard peaks of her nipples visible under her sweater.

"We'd better get going. Pack whatever's essential and we'll buy anything else when we get there."

He saw the flash of confusion in her eyes at his brusque manner, then she crossed her arms over her waist and nodded. "It'll only take me a minute." She raised one hand to gesture at his face. "I'm sorry about that."

Emelio thought about his parents, about the closeness and caring they all took for granted. "I'm sorry that your family let you down."

Stevie's blue eyes turned clear and cold. "The people you trust to protect you always hurt you the most."

Her words sliced into him like a razor as she turned to go inside the apartment. The guilt that bled out of his heart made him even more determined to keep her safe at all costs.

He thought about his dead informant. He wasn't going to make the same mistakes with Stevie. He had to concentrate on hunting down Braga before *he* found *them.* It was the only way to protect her.

Emelio went back inside the apartment and closed the French doors behind him. Looking around at the destruction strengthened his resolve. *Gracias a Dios,* she hadn't been home. She might have ended up in the same condition. He looked at his watch and called out.

"Get it in gear, Stevie."

"I'm coming."

He heard a drawer bang in the bedroom and sighed. If she was anything like his sisters, Stevie's idea of essential differed greatly from his. While he waited, his eyes catalogued her belongings, storing the information of her likes and preferences. The corners of his mouth twitched in amusement when he noticed she had the complete collection of James Bond videos.

A gleam of white caught his eye and he saw something partly hidden beneath the cane-back chair. His gaze narrowed to a sharp focus when he noticed a dark shadow along the top. There was something familiar about that pattern....

As Emelio turned the chair over, he saw that the object wasn't white but pearl gray. He could only stare at the box of stationery with a black-lace design embossed on the edge. He reached for the envelope in his back pocket, comparing them to be certain.

Stevie? Stevie was the mystery woman who'd been mailing him erotic notes for almost four months?

At the office, she was friendly but professional. She was straightforward and hardworking and…sexy as hell. He suddenly remembered the flirtatious sparkle in her eyes when she sat on the edge of his desk earlier. She must have seen black-lace letter number nine in the stack of mail.

Stevie was his secret seductress.

Words that she'd written in the second letter flashed across his mind.

> I straddle my thighs over your lap, my mouth open to your hot, wet kisses as I unbutton your shirt. Your hands glide under my skirt, pulling me closer to the hard bulge of your jeans….

Not only did he remember every sentence from every letter, but he also realized that they were going to be roommates for an indefinite amount of time. Emelio groaned out loud. He'd been fighting his attraction to her before. How the hell was he going to keep his hands off of her now?

3

"ALLIGATOR... ALLIGATOR... Oh, look...more alligators."

Emelio changed his grip on the steering wheel and glanced over at Stevie. Her short blond hair was tousled from the wind blowing into Alex's Jeep as they headed due west along U.S. 41 towards Naples, Florida. One elbow was propped on the open window, her chin resting on her palm. She stared out at the large reptiles sunning themselves beside the canal that ran next to the road.

He chuckled at her petulant tone. "Come on, it's not all 'gators. I saw a couple of herons and a deer."

"Too bad the 'gators didn't eat the deer. It would have broken up the monotony." Stevie let out a long-suffering and exaggerated sigh.

"You could use a little boredom today." He reached over to turn the radio on low.

She sighed again, squirming a little in her seat. Her movements caused the short blue-and-white skirt to ride up, exposing more of her long, shapely legs. His fingers itched to reach out and stroke the smooth, tanned skin, feel the lean muscle just below the surface.

The next song on the radio was a slow sexy ballad. *I'll make love to you, baby, all through the night—*

He flicked a button to change the radio station. That

song was not what he needed to hear right now. Instead, he focused on the flat, tree-lined road ahead, stretching out as endless and hot as Stevie's legs.... He had to stop daydreaming and pay attention to the highway.

This section of U.S. 41 had no emergency shoulder, just a crumbling edge immediately bordering the wetlands. It wouldn't take much for the Jeep to end up among the palmettos and waist-high saw grass. Every time he made this trip from Miami, he got the feeling that if he stopped for too long, the fecund greenery would sprout up and make him an unwilling part of the Everglades.

Stevie dropped her arm off the window ledge and into her lap with another irritated sigh. Hiding an amused smirk, he braced for her next harangue.

"If you'd let me drive—"

"Forget it, Jayne Bond."

"—I would have gone up to Route I-75. The interstate is a lot faster."

He adjusted his sunglasses against the glare of the midday sun. "Maybe. But it would have been harder to keep track of the vehicles around us."

Stevie crossed her arms under her perfect breasts and grumbled sarcastically. "No problem here. We've been on this two-lane, mosquito infested highway following the same slow-moving minivan for the last thirty miles."

He silently agreed. His frustration levels had risen along with the time spent on the road, too. If they had taken the interstate, it would have only been a two-hour drive across the state. But after changing cars again, he'd decided the Tamiami Trail through Big Cypress Nature Preserve would be the safer of the two choices.

"Relax. It's a nice day. The sun is shining. Try to enjoy the beauty that's all around us."

"It's a swamp, Emelio." The whine of the cicadas rose to a crescendo as if to emphasize her words. "All I see is kudzu vines, scrub pine and more goddamn alligators."

She'd probably smack him, but not even her foul mood could detract from her appeal. "You know, you're very cute when you're complaining."

Stevie inclined her head, regarding him with a quirk of one eyebrow. "Are you flirting with me?"

"No, of course not."

He shouldn't be flirting. But it was hard to remain aloof when black-lace letter number nine lay on the console between them. Every now and again, he noticed her glance down at the envelope and then over at him. He couldn't wait to find out what was written inside. Maybe he'd ask her to read it to him. Out loud, in that sexy Southern drawl that caressed his senses and danced along his nerves. Maybe she'd be naked, too.

Stevie sat up straight and stared at him. "Your lips moved."

"What?"

"I saw your lips move. Careful, Emelio. That was almost a grin. With teeth and everything."

It had been a long time since he'd felt like smiling, and yet Stevie had brought him close twice today. He decided not to comment, not sure himself what it meant.

"Didn't you even realize you'd let it slip? No?

That's my new mission, then. To do whatever it takes to get you to smile again."

Whatever it took? Images from her seductive notes crowded his thoughts.

> The feel of my bare breasts rubbing against your chest makes my pulse race. Then you pull me into your embrace, your hands gliding down my naked body as you lower your mouth to my waiting lips....

Thinking about the possibilities was enough to strain the placket of his jeans. "That could be interpreted as sexual harassment, you know."

"My, my. What made you jump to that conclusion?" Her laugh was darkly sensual, and her accent slipped into the cadence of her native New Orleans. "Don't worry, *chér.* You'll know right sure when I start harassing you."

You know you want me. I know it, too—

The suggestive lyrics on the radio echoed his thoughts and increased the tension within the small space of the Jeep. Emelio switched the station again. Damn, what was it with the music today?

Give in to the feelin', 'cause you're gonna be mine—

He clicked the radio off.

Stevie looked over, amusement glowing in her eyes. "Is something wrong, Emelio?"

"Nope. I'd just rather listen to the mosquitoes and cicadas."

She laughed again, low and husky, as the car phone rang. Emelio picked up the earpiece so the caller wouldn't be on the speaker. Alex's voice rumbled in his ear.

"I'm on vacation, hombre. What are you paging me for and what the hell are you doing in my Jeep?"

"Sorry, man. I had to take your wheels to get out of town."

Alex's tone instantly became serious. "Talk to me."

"The Dominican cartel sent a message. It came through the office, but somehow Stevie is involved." Emelio was well aware she was openly listening to his end of the conversation.

"Shit. How bad is it?"

He debated less than a second about how much to say. "How soon can you get back?"

His friend blew out a breath. "I'll be on the next plane from Baltimore."

"We're heading for José's place. You can reach me there. And Alex..."

"You're welcome. Just watch your back, since I can't be there to do it."

Stevie settled her sunglasses on her nose to hide the fire she knew was blazing in her eyes. Her temper idled between *annoyed* and *aggravated* while she waited for Emelio to finish the call. How was she supposed to solve her first case, her own case, if he kept withholding information?

"Now that you've let Alex in on what's happening—"

"Alex is my partner. While I keep you safe in Naples, he's going to be digging around in Miami. And not without considerable risk, since he testified against the cartel, too." He reached up to turn the visor down over the windshield, his sunglasses apparently not enough defense against the glare.

Alex wasn't his only partner from now on. She was

damned sick of being patted on the head as if she couldn't be trusted. She was smart and strong and determined to be included.

"Then let me tell you what *I* know, Emelio. A hundred million dollars is a lot of money, but to a drug trafficking organization, it's a drop in a very big bucket. That means the cartel's message can only be personal. And I'm betting it has something to do with the man you tried to get me to recognize in that one photo."

With his eyes hidden, there was no way to gauge his expression, but she saw his lips thin and noticed his hands gripped the steering wheel a little tighter.

"Information is knowledge, Emelio, and knowledge—"

"—will often get you killed. You're too smart for your own good, Stevie." His tone suggested a reluctant admiration.

She immediately latched on to his words. "I heard Alex say once that Overtown was the end of your career with Justice. Who got killed?"

He drew in a deep breath and very slowly exhaled through pursed lips. Then he surprised her by giving a direct answer. "The man in the photo is Rogelio Braga, Frankie Ramos's replacement."

"What happened in Overtown?"

For a long while he didn't reply. He gingerly rubbed the bruise on his jaw, concentrating on the road. "An informant I'd used to get evidence against the cartel double-crossed our team during a bogus drug buy. When the bullets started flying, she was killed in the gunfire."

Stevie wondered if he realized how much was given away by the undercurrent in his voice. However things had gone wrong, Emelio obviously blamed himself. And her instincts told her he was still holding something back, so she hit him with the question that was uppermost on her mind.

"Why is Braga threatening me?"

He was quiet for a few seconds and she could almost feel his withdrawal. Then he shook his head. "I don't know yet."

Her voice hardened as she stared at him. "Take a wild guess."

"Like you said, information is knowledge." Emelio's eyebrows drew together. "The question is, what does he think you know?"

ROGELIO BRAGA SLAMMED his fist against the oak surface of his desk. Bloody useless fools!

Frustration mingled with disgust and had him moving to the wet bar to pour a tumbler of dark rum. One of his first tasks when his takeover was complete would be to reorganize. He would eliminate anyone who dared substandard performance. Incompetence could not, and would not, be tolerated under the new regime.

The thug he'd hired from outside the cartel to take care of the Madison woman had failed him. He managed to deliver the messages, but had stupidly taken it upon himself to ravage her apartment, thereby alerting her to the extent of her peril before he'd planned. Then, not only had he lost them in traffic, he'd ended up in hospital. Braga would see to it he never left.

He swallowed a mouthful of the rum, hissing through his teeth as its fire trickled down his throat. He had bigger problems than the messenger.

His former boss, Frankie Ramos, had been offered

the chance to make a deal in exchange for information about the cartel. Ramos was going to spill his guts in the courtroom unless Braga spilled them first. But so far none of his people had been able to find out where Ramos was being held.

Braga slumped into his wing chair, splashing rum against the side of the tumbler. He refused to settle for less than total control. He would find the woman and he would find Ramos. It was time to call in an old and very valuable debt. There had been small favors over the years—recanting witnesses, "lost" evidence—but now something more was required.

EMELIO GUIDED the Jeep along the main street through the Old Naples section of the city. The picturesque Fifth Avenue South was crowded with people strolling along the landscaped promenades or lunching in one of the many open-air cafés. He felt the tension ease from his shoulders. Only his family and best friend knew he stayed here, so he and Stevie should be safe from Braga's spies.

He loved vacationing here, loved the escape from everyday life the quaint Gulf Coast town offered. Stevie's head swiveled from side to side, her gaze trying to take in everything at once. Emelio knew how she felt. No matter how often he came here, the city's charm and grace still affected him.

Old Naples boasted a low skyline of pastel-painted stucco-and-glass buildings tucked among palm trees and lush foliage. Upscale boutiques nestled beside jewelry stores and antique shops. Each structure was uniquely designed with columns or archways, recessed plazas with murmuring fountains and flower-draped balconies.

Stevie pointed to a series of six-foot fiberglass reptiles decorating the sand-colored brick sidewalks. "I can't get away from the alligators."

Emelio chuckled. "Those are part of the 'Gators Galore' public art project. It's to raise money for the Boys and Girls Club. Kind of like the 'Fish Out of Water' project in Baltimore and the 'Cows on Parade' in Chicago."

"They dress better than the gators back in the swamp. I like that one over there, with the sparkly purple evening gown, pink shoes and gold eyelashes."

As he breathed in the scent of warm sea air and tropical flowers, he made a right turn onto Gulf Shore Boulevard. He immediately felt the cool breeze coming off the greenish-blue water. Glancing to his left as he drove, he could catch glimpses of the sugar-white sandy beach. Only a few more minutes and he'd be home.

Funny that he thought of it that way. Mamá, Pápi and his sisters lived within walking distance of his house in Coral Gables. His parents' house was always full of relatives and friends, music and raised voices and his family was the most important thing in the world to him.

And yet… All of that love and togetherness could be stifling at times.

As the firstborn and the only son of Cuban immigrants, he carried the burden of responsibility and parental expectation. From the earliest age, Mamá and Pápi instilled in him a strong sense of family, honor and duty. How could he face his family if they ever found out that his informant, a woman he was responsible for, had been killed? He'd never allow that to happen ever again.

Still, he looked over at Stevie and wondered if he'd made the best decision by bringing her to Naples. Of course, he knew it was right—he had to protect her—but his chest tightened with more than a little resentment over having to take her to the beachside cottage. It was his solace, his sanctuary, and in taking her there he'd have to reveal his secret perhaps.

Then he remembered the mess in her apartment, and the look of devastation in her eyes when she saw it. He'd made the only decision he could. Keeping Stevie safe from harm was his chance to regain his honor, a belated attempt to make things right again, to find some peace.

Stevie's belly rumbled and she turned her attention from the scenery to the matter at hand. "I'm starving. Can we stop somewhere for burgers and onion rings?"

"Sorry. There are a lot of cafés and restaurants in Old Naples, but no fast-food places."

She stared at him in disbelief. "No golden arches, no yellow bells, no red-and-white buckets? How am I supposed to survive?"

"That stuff is poison. We'll stop by the grocers and I'll make us an early dinner."

Half an hour later, Emelio guided the Jeep through the security gates of an exclusive resort community. Stevie's eyebrows shot up and she yanked her sunglasses off. Not many private detectives traveled in the kind of circles that allowed them to stay in a place like this.

After passing several streets, he turned onto a circular driveway shaded by a canopy of palm trees.

Behind a wrought-iron gate, the butter-beige stucco walls and white tile roof of the Bermuda-style house gleamed in the late afternoon sun. The front formed a U-shape with tall mullioned windows overlooking the central courtyard.

Stevie looked from the house to Emelio and back. "I thought you said your friend had a 'cottage'?"

He shrugged. "That's what the realtor called it."

"Hiding from deranged drug-dealing stalkers won't be so bad after all."

Emelio pulled onto a parking pad beside one of the sandstone gateposts and shut off the engine. He took off his own sunglasses and gazed over at the house with a pensive expression for a moment. Then he climbed out of the Jeep and walked toward the cargo section. "I'll get the groceries."

Stevie opened her door and got out, as well. She took only a few steps before her heel twisted on the crushed shells and gravel. In an instant, Emelio was there, cupping her elbow to steady her. His large hands felt warm and strong, and she ached to feel them on her naked body. When their eyes met, she saw the awareness mirrored in his gaze.

Would he kiss her again? The memory of that first contact had been seared onto her lips. With little effort, she recalled the shock of desire and need, the feel of his hard, aroused body against hers. But even as she waited for a repeat experience, Emelio stepped back. Though a twinge of disappointment settled in her chest, she didn't push. She was willing to bide her time and she'd bet he was worth waiting for.

She followed the driveway, carefully picking her way on the high-heeled sandals. He reached over to the gatepost and pushed one of the sandstone cobbles aside. When he punched in a sequence of numbers on the hidden security keypad, the tall iron gates slid silently apart.

"Wow. So this is Golden Eye." When he glanced over with a curious expression, she explained. "Ian Fleming's tropical hideaway. He wrote most of the Bond books there."

Amusement lit the hazel depths of his eyes. Emelio lowered his voice to a confidential whisper. "Wait until you see the secret laboratory of spy gadgets hidden in the cave under the dining room."

Stevie laughed as they walked along the pathway leading to the front door. The courtyard was landscaped on either side with dark green palmetto, sweetly scented Indian blanket, graceful sword fern and lantana in shades of purple and violet. Alone in this fabulous house, miles and miles away from danger, she could let her attraction and his interest take the natural course. Mr. Calm, Cool and Controlled wouldn't know what hit him.

A tendril of doubt curled in her belly, but she shoved it aside. She wasn't Tom's insecure and intimidated little wife anymore. That was all behind her. She'd found the courage to leave, the will to fight him for a divorce and the guts to move to a strange city and start her life over.

After that, confessing to Emelio that she'd written the letters would be a breeze.

When he shifted one of the grocery bags to his side, Stevie took it from him to hold. He flipped through the keys on his ring, and then fit one into each of the two locks on the front door.

"You just happen to have the keys already?"

"I stay here as often as I can."

He stood aside to let her go past, her heels rapping against the terra-cotta tiles. Stevie looked around the simply decorated entrance foyer, noting that the house felt smaller than it had looked from the outside. A hallway stretched the length of the house to a back door, with arched entryways on either side that led to the rooms of the house.

Stevie set the bag down on the smoked-glass accent table in the foyer. She watched as Emelio swung the mirror above it open and fiddled with yet another security system. "What happens if you put in the wrong top-secret code?"

"Bambi and Thumper show up and beat the crap out of me."

Her brows furrowed in confusion. "Those cute little Disney animals?"

Emelio looked at her, sympathy coloring his tone. "You must be tired. Thumper and Bambi were the two bad girls who tried to kill Bond in *Diamonds Are Forever.*"

"Oh, yeah. I love that scene. They all end up wrestling in the swimming pool." She cocked her head to one side and crossed her arms. "I think we got off the subject, though. Whose house is this really?"

His features darkened, closing off his expression. "It's mine, Stevie."

"But you told Alex we were going to—"

The words died in her throat and her arms dropped to her sides when she caught sight of the living room. Her eyes widened as she walked closer.

"Watch the step." Emelio caught her elbow again before she tripped, then leaned one shoulder against the archway, both hands shoved into his front pockets.

She barely heard him, only vaguely noting the cathedral ceiling and large windows and that the room had the same stark modernist décor as his office back in Miami. Her gaze was focused on the José Castillo paintings displayed on every pale beige wall.

Stevie knew her art, having grown up with a collection that had been handed down through the generations. She especially knew Castillo's work since he was her favorite modern painter. But she'd never seen any of these works in a book or gallery catalogue.

"These are originals, aren't they? These paintings have never been shown outside of this house, have they?" Her voice rose with each question as she dashed from frame to frame to frame in disbelief. "These are *your* paintings!"

He answered in a monotone. "So now you know my secret."

"But how—?"

"My full name is Emelio José Castillo Sanchez."

She finally turned to look at him. A scowl twisted his full lips even as patches of color reddened his cheeks.

"Come on. After I put the groceries away, I'll show you the house."

Stevie dogged his footsteps into the large, sunny kitchen. "I can't believe it. Emelio, you're a wonderful artist, one of the most talented in the world. Why would you keep something like this to yourself?"

Emelio kept his back to her as he filled the refrigerator. "Everybody has secrets, don't they, Stevie."

"I told you mine back at my apartment."

"Not all of them."

Well, he had her there. But some things about her

past were better left in the past. After throwing the grocery bag away, he crossed to the other side of the kitchen, not waiting to see if she followed, which, of course, she did.

"This is the Florida room." He waved one arm to encompass a large tiled sunroom. Floor-to-ceiling glass offered a perfect view of the blue-green Gulf waves lapping against the powder-white sand. Despite the gorgeous panorama, she wasn't about to be distracted.

"I admire those paintings in your office every time I come in, you've never said a word. When were you going to tell me?"

"I wasn't. No one outside of my family knows except Alex and my agent. And now you. That's the way I want it." He unlocked the French doors and slid them open to access the glass-walled room that enclosed the swimming pool.

She followed him out to the lanai, stepping around one of the lounge chairs as she walked. "I still can't believe you're José Castillo. Your work is incredible! It's provocative and passionate and yet you're so..."

He stopped to glance over his shoulder, curiosity lacing his tone. "So what?"

"Well...inhibited."

Emelio arched one raven-wing eyebrow, as if she'd insulted him, and for one brief instant his heated gaze stripped her bare. A jolt of electric awareness danced along her spine, hardening her nipples before settling between her thighs.

"Whoa. What was that look?"

"What look, Stevie?" When he shifted his weight to one leg and shoved his hands into his back pockets, the pistachio cotton of his shirt tightened across his broad shoulders.

"That look you just gave me." Stevie ran her tongue over her lower lip and sashayed over to his side. Like a Bond babe going after classified documents, she felt the heat and turned it up fifty degrees. Tilting her head playfully, she reached out to draw one finger over the hard planes of his chest.

Strands of thick coffee hair fell over his forehead, luring her attention to the gleam of mischief and more that lit his eyes. The edge of his mouth curved and he lowered his voice to an intimate purr. "I was just wondering... When were you going to tell me you wrote the black-lace letters?"

Stevie gasped out a nervous laugh as her heart skittered to a halt, then pounded back to life. "Is that what you call them? I hadn't figured out how to tell you. When did you know?"

"I saw the stationery in your living room." He tipped his face down, his gaze focused on her mouth. "Like I said, we all have secrets."

"Now that it's out in the open, and we have this place all to ourselves, what are we going to do about it?"

Emelio held utterly still, in that watchful and predatory manner she'd come to know. But his eyes gave him away. Staring into the depths of his amber-green gaze, Stevie knew she had reached him on a primal level at last. She drew closer, seducing him with her eyes, yearning for another taste of his kiss.

Then a shutter came down over his features. He reached up to sweep the hair from his forehead, looking around as if he'd just remembered where they were. Regret darkened his eyes a second before he raised his chin and stepped away.

"I have a strict policy against workplace relationships."

He walked along the edge of the swimming pool to the other side of the room and punched in a code for the back door. From the main hallway, another arch led to the short hall of the private section of the house. He flicked one hand toward the room on the right. "This is the gym."

Stevie leaned around him, making sure her breasts brushed across his arm, and glanced inside. Expensive-looking boxing equipment and weight sets lined the padded mat-covered floor. She studied his reflection in the mirrored panels. "We're nowhere near the agency now."

In the mirror, his eyes widened at the contact and for an instant she saw his desire. He shifted back on his heels and jammed his fists into his pockets. A residual sheen of lust still clouded his gaze, but his tone was decisive. "You still work for me, Stevie."

"Okay. I quit."

"Resignation duly noted," he said wryly. "But the policy is in place for a reason. Sleeping with someone who works for you impairs your judgment."

"So who said anything about sleep?"

His nostrils flared and she saw his pupils dilate. She was standing close enough to hear the quick intake of breath before he shook his head. "Even if I accepted your resignation, which I don't, that doesn't solve anything. You asked me to take you on as a new client. The same policy applies."

"Not a problem. You're fired."

He crossed his arms and straightened to his full

height. ''Nice try, Stevie, but you can't fire me. We never actually contracted the job so—''

''So I'm not really a client and you have no more excuses.'' She batted her eyelashes and grinned at him.

A myriad of reactions hurtled across his face, too swiftly for her to interpret any of them, but she could tell he was vacillating. Stevie turned, heading toward the opposite end of the passageway, noting a full bath and an office as she walked by. The last door opened onto a master-bedroom suite. A large side window looked out at the lanai and a set of French doors opened onto a brick-walled patio with a hot tub in the center.

Then she focused on the room and realized there was only a king-size four-poster with an elaborately carved mahogany headboard, no other furniture. Hoo yah. The ''cottage'' had only one real bedroom. And only one bed.

Though the carpeting muffled his steps, she knew instantly that Emelio had walked up behind her. The air was suddenly charged with a restless energy, and the faint citrus and spice of his cologne drifted to her senses.

Gazing at the paintings on the walls, large abstract images of brightly swirling colors, she wondered why Emelio kept this other, boldly sensual part of his personality hidden. Obviously his art was his emotional outlet, the only way he could really express himself.

Well, she'd just have to show him another method....

4

STEVIE TURNED AND SAUNTERED toward him, a purposeful gleam in her slate-blue eyes. The sexual heat in her gaze hit him hard and he knew he was in trouble.

She raised her arms, draping them behind his neck. He could feel her hardened nipples through the material of her sweater, and the heat of her body underneath. His heart knocked crazily in his chest. Her lush mouth slowly parted, moist and inviting. He had an instant to take a shuddering breath.

And then he was lost.

He reached for her, tracing his tongue over the fullness of her broad lower lip. She opened to him, deepening the kiss. Emelio slanted his mouth over hers, drinking in her sweetness as she wound her arms tighter about his neck. The taste of her was like liquid fire in his veins. Until he heard the sound.

Either Stevie's stomach was growling again or a late-season hurricane was rumbling toward the coast.

Some of the sexual tension eased, but a current still crackled between them. He gently stroked her upper arm, oddly grateful that her protesting belly had broken the mood. Whether or not to sleep...have sex with Stevie was a decision he couldn't make lightly, but lust was overshadowing logic. Despite the reasons and protests he'd just offered, he was tempted, very tempted.

They stood facing each other, both intently aware that the bed was only a few steps away. Pulse thudding, his resolve wavered dangerously as he met her aggressive look. She was so beautiful, so sure of herself, and he definitely wanted—

Her belly rumbled again. She laughed, ducking her chin, and pressed one hand against her abdomen. "I told you I was starving."

"Guess I'd better start cooking, then. Those tuna steaks won't take long, so dinner should be ready in about twenty-five minutes."

"Thanks. If you don't mind, I'd like to freshen up. I feel all…hot and sticky."

She smiled innocently at him, but the invitation in her eyes was as bad as could be. Difficult as it was, he ignored the bait. It wasn't her stomach's moans he wanted to hear when he finally took her to bed.

"I'll get your bag so you can change."

Not until he stepped out the front door, achingly conscious of the erection pressing against his zipper, did Emelio realize his choice had already been made. Just now, he'd thought "when," not "if," he should take Stevie to bed.

He paused in the courtyard, his distracted gaze turned inward. His primary mission was to guard Stevie against Braga. He was supposed to consider her both an employee and a client. The trouble was, right now, he could only think of her as a beautiful and enticing siren.

Emelio opened the door to the Jeep and saw black-lace letter number nine still resting on the console between the front seats. Hell, who was he kidding?

The decision to get involved with her had been made, at least subconsciously, when he found out she was his secret seductress.

Her provocative words had occupied both his dreams and waking thoughts for months. A sharp pang of pure lust gripped him as he added Stevie's face and body to the erotic scenes in his head.... He grabbed the letter, pulled her travel bag and his gun case out of the cargo area and headed back to the house.

After dropping his Ruger Mark II in the office, he strode down the hall to give Stevie her clothes. He'd just remembered there were no clean towels in the master bath. On his way to the bedroom, he grabbed some from the linen closet. Hopefully, he could catch her before—

Her sandals had been kicked off near the bed. Her sweater was in a puddle on the carpet, a lace bra and her blue-and-white skirt nearby. And her panties, her black-lace thong panties, lay just outside the bathroom door.

Emelio set the suitcase by the walk-in closet while he debated what to do with the towels tucked under his arm. Bound by the cardinal rules of sharing a house with three sisters, he rapped lightly on the door before turning the knob. He'd just drop the towels on the chair for her.

He started to speak but the words caught in his throat. Late-afternoon sun glimmered softly through the window behind the shower, highlighting Stevie's profile against the frosted-glass door. He could only stare, his eyes burning from the effort to focus her body into more than a long silhouette of tantalizing curves.

The words from black-lace letter number three came back to taunt him.

I love the way you watch me, the way your eyes slowly roam over my body. It makes me hot…and so very wet. Come closer and feel for yourself.

"Temptation" ought to be her middle name. His heart pounded erratically as he continued to look his fill and, in that instant, Emelio was no longer her employer or her protector. He was simply a man who wanted a woman.

STEVIE STOOD BENEATH the spray so that the three separate showerheads pulsated against the base of her skull, between her shoulder blades and over her lower back.

She let her mind empty of all thoughts except the feel of the shower cascading down her body, imagining the last of her fear and emotional stress washing away with the hot water. She was safe; she was with Emelio. Nothing else mattered right now.

Then she felt it, the slightest hint of cool air brushing her skin. Subtly tilting her head, Stevie opened her eyes, squinting through the steamy frosted glass until she could just make out a shadowy figure in the doorway. Listening intently, she tried to make out the click of the door closing back into place—or better yet the thump of denim jeans hitting the floor. But she only heard the water splashing against the glass blocks.

How long had Emelio been standing there? Her heart stuttered as a combination of embarrassment and mischief zinged through her veins. The third note she'd written to him involved the idea of him watching her. A wild and wicked impulse overcame her, urging her to bring that fantasy to life.

She reached for the massaging showerhead at the top of the pole, pulling it down by the metal coil. Positioning herself directly in front of the opaque glass window so the golden-orange sunshine backlit her body, she turned the dial from gentle throb to jet propulsion.

Holding the sprayer in one hand, she slid the other over her chest to cup her right breast, then played the hot pulsating water across it. A gasp escaped her throat when she directed the stream to drum against the sensitive peak, causing a tugging contraction deep in her belly.

From beneath half-closed lids, she made sure that Emelio was still watching from the doorway. She couldn't be certain, but she thought she'd heard his footsteps edging closer. Bracing her back on the wall, her head resting against the window, Stevie slowly lowered the sprayer. As silky hot water hammered her body, the ripple and clutch of sexual need almost brought her to her knees.

Her uninhibited moan echoed through the shower stall when the wet heat blasted the core of her need. The insistent throb became a delicious ache and she felt her belly quiver and tighten as the climax built inside her.

The pleasure was too intense, too fast, and she came instantly. The ragged sound of her breathing filled the room as the rush of satisfaction slowly ebbed. Moments later, she replaced the showerhead on its hook and returned the dial to the fine mist setting while her heart rate returned to normal.

A loud knock startled her and she swung her head toward the bathroom door. Why was he knocking? She hadn't imagined the shadow in the doorway. "Yes?"

Emelio cleared his throat, then said, "Clean towels," in a voice as husky as her own. Holding back a laugh, Stevie wondered if he was smiling yet.

"YOU'RE A MAN OF MANY TALENTS, Emelio. I never would have guessed you were this good."

"Well, I figured we needed something quick but satisfying."

When she brushed a damp tendril of hair off her cheek, he thought about her shower. Watching Stevie indulge herself was the sexiest thing he'd ever seen. And hearing her breathy little gasps had increased the heavy, aching pressure in his groin to the point of discomfort. He'd never wanted a woman so badly in his life.

A teasing light shone in Stevie's azure eyes as she looked over at him. "The faster, the better. But I didn't think you liked it that way."

"I do prefer to take my time, but I knew you were hungry so I rushed."

She looked beautiful in the red-gold colors of twilight streaming through the window. Her bare skin was still flushed with heat, and she seemed relaxed for the first time all day, as if her usual energetic intensity had been ratcheted down a few notches. She proved him right by yawning.

"Sorry. I didn't sleep much last night."

She looked ready for bed, dressed in a faded pink

T-shirt and a pair of yoga pants that flared over her bare feet. Despite the casual attire, she was incredibly sexy and it required superhuman effort to keep from staring at her breasts. Her perfect, round, bouncy, not-wearing-a-bra…

Emelio nodded toward the food-laden plates set on the dining table. "Go ahead and take a seat."

"Everything looks wonderful. What is it?" Her chair scraped lightly over the ceramic-tile floor as she pulled it aside.

He called out his reply from the kitchen while choosing a bottle from the wine cooler next to the refrigerator. "Ahi tuna in a blood-orange teriyaki sauce, long-grain and wild rice with mushrooms and a field-greens salad with blue cheese and winter pears."

"Mmm, yummy. You know, unless you count frozen pizza, I've never had a guy cook for me before."

Emelio walked back into the dining room with the wine in one hand and two goblets balanced in the other. "Well, there's a first time for—"

The smile melted from Stevie's lips, the vivid color fading from her cheeks. Her gaze narrowed, focused on the wine bottle like a laser. The expression on her face was one he imagined a drowning man wore when he spotted a life vest.

"I can get us something else, Stevie." Her features had returned to normal, but her eyes hadn't left the wine.

"You don't have to. I mean, don't let me keep you from enjoying it. Domaine D'Or pouilly-fumé, right? They make an excellent sauvignon blanc, also." A strained silence followed while she ducked her head and concentrated on her meal.

"How long have you been sober?"

She didn't answer straightaway. "It never became that much of a problem. I just used to have a couple glasses of wine at night.... I don't drink anymore." She tried to keep her tone light, hoping he heard the pride and not the regret.

"I'll be right back." He pivoted and headed for the kitchen. He returned a moment later with two glasses of sparkling water and took the seat to her left at the table. "Here you go."

"You're learning all of my secrets today, aren't you?"

A sip of water did little to wash the taste of failure from her mouth. Stevie clenched one hand into a tight fist in her lap and finally raised her eyes to meet his. If she focused on his face, maybe the image of that chilled, straw-yellow bottle would disappear and take the fierce longing for a taste, just one little sip, away with it. His enigmatic gaze was, as always, non-judgmental.

"After Overtown, Alex had to come and pull me out of a couple bars when I knew better than to drive home."

She nodded her head, acknowledging what he'd said as well as the message behind his words. It was that understanding that allowed her to explain. "Everyone kept telling me how lucky I was, what a great life I had. So when Tom would fly into a rage, it must have been my fault somehow, right?"

She forced a bite of fish between cold lips, still haunted by the wine's false comfort. The weight of remembered emotion dropped onto her shoulders, adding to her fatigue.

"I was so alone, you know? So scared and depressed. One drink led to a second and a third... For a while I thought it was an escape. But actually it was a crutch, and something else for Tom to use against me."

Emelio had given up all pretense of eating. He draped one arm over the back of his chair and just listened. "What finally gave you the courage to walk away?"

"He started hitting me. He was careful to hit me where no one could see, where the bruises wouldn't show in public. Then I 'fell' and ended up in the hospital." Stevie dropped her gaze with a bitter twist of her mouth.

"I was lucky that Dr. Weitzman had some experience dealing with what she called Painful Privilege. Apparently there are a lot of successful, well-educated women who are battered by their powerful, high-profile husbands. With Dr. Weitzman's help and some therapy, I filed for divorce."

"I can't imagine how...difficult...that must have been for you." Again, Emelio seemed to look beneath the surface and understand what she didn't say.

Difficult didn't begin to describe the final months of her marriage. She touched a finger to the bridge of her nose, a permanent reminder of Tom's reaction to the divorce papers.

With therapy, she'd learned to look to the future instead of dwelling on the past. She'd gotten a one-time settlement instead of alimony just to make sure all ties to New Orleans were broken. Thinking about better times, she did her best to lighten the mood. Frankly, she'd had enough of memory lane for one day.

"It was worth it. I got my life back. And, believe

me, I really lived it up for a while. Kind of acted like a kid who's been grounded for a couple months."

"Oh, yeah. How?" Reading her mood, Emelio picked up his fork and speared a mouthful of his salad.

Stevie laughed and shook her head. "The story of my wild and rebellious postmarital days is staying a secret."

"I'll tell you about my wild days if you tell about yours."

"Please. A little earring isn't what I would consider outrageous." With renewed appetite, she plowed into the fish and rice on her plate.

He touched a finger to the sapphire stud in his left ear. "I'd just been assigned to the Special Operations Division. Alex had worked undercover before and he figured I needed something to make me look street-wise. It was either this or get a tattoo."

"I have a tattoo."

His dark eyebrows lifted and his expression was one of fascinated disbelief. "What is it? *Where* is it?"

"I've got a purple-and-black butterfly." A spark of mischief ignited inside her and she let a slow, inviting smile spread across her face. "But you'll have to find it yourself."

"It might require a very thorough search."

The melodic timbre of his voice turned his statement into a promise and sent her pulse into overdrive. Sensual awareness leaped between them as Emelio let his eyes travel slowly over her body, as if the intense heat of his gaze would burn away her clothing and reveal the tattoo.

"Now are you flirting with me, Emelio?"

"Yes. I am."

Stevie's eyebrows arched in surprise. Well, hot damn. Or maybe it was that hot shower. "What made you change your mind?"

He shrugged one broad shoulder, as if making light of the situation, but the intensity of his expression gave him away. "Your black-lace letters. A man can only take so much teasing, and, lady, you've been tempting me for too long."

"But?"

One corner of his mouth curved slightly, as if he was amused by how easily she'd read him. Then the teasing light faded from his eyes. "But first we need to talk."

Stevie groaned and dropped her chin. "Don't get all serious on me. We've had enough depressing discussions for one day."

Emelio reached over to take her hand. "I have to consider what happens when we get back to Miami, how our employment relationship is going to be affected."

She leaned forward, pleased when his eyes glanced down at her cleavage. "I thought we settled the issue when I fired you."

"This is important, Stevie. You work for me and, at the moment, I'm protecting you. We don't know what Braga wants from you or how long we're going to be here."

He hesitated, as though weighing his next words. "Typically, in circumstances like this, undercover assignments or witness protection or whatever, time seems compressed, emotions run high. When you're on a case, you've got to constantly remember it's not real life."

"How romantic." Stevie pulled her hand away and

sat back in her chair. It seemed he was ending things before they'd even started, and she didn't like feeling the tiny stab of rejection.

Emelio kept his tone professionally remote, but blatant desire lit his hazel eyes. "Romance has nothing to do with it—it's about two people giving in to irresistible possibility."

"Gee, Emelio, try not to be so excited."

He reached for her again, his expression earnest, and the heat of his skin penetrated her hand. "Believe me, I am turned on. I want to fulfill your fantasies, and maybe create some new ones with you."

Wisps of heat raced along her nerves and desire tickled its way down her body. He was saying the words she'd longed to hear, but she saw the residual uncertainty all too clearly on his face. Something twisted inside her at the thought of their relationship going no further than the physical.

"So, what's the problem?"

"All I'm saying is, with forced proximity, relationships that normally take months to develop can happen in a matter of hours. I don't want to make the mistake— Neither of us should be rushing into anything beyond an exploration of desire."

She'd had the hots for him practically from the moment they'd met, so she didn't exactly think of it as rushing. But obviously, for a guy who was juggling three other women, getting romantically involved with her was a real dilemma.

Even knowing she shouldn't fall for another charismatic, take-charge male, Stevie was more than willing to explore this powerful attraction then take it to the next level. But it would scare him off if she voiced her feelings now. So outwardly she gave a little shrug and smiled, falling back on the nonchalant cadence of her native Louisiana.

"Sure thing, chér. We'll pass a good time then see what happens."

"I knew you'd understand."

He relaxed visibly and gently tugged her hand until she came over to sit on his lap. The proof of his desire was hard beneath her thigh. There was no doubt that he wanted her, but for how long? Stevie slid one arm behind his neck and smiled.

"Did you enjoy the latest note I sent you?"

"I haven't opened it yet."

She arched one eyebrow in surprise. "Really? Why not?"

His gaze was magnetic, drawing her in with its seductive promise. "Anticipation is the second-best part of seduction."

"Yeah, but why settle for second best?" She tilted her head to one side, flirting with him from beneath her lashes. "Don't you even want a hint about the letter?"

"Nope. When the time comes, I want you to read it to me. Naked."

Stevie felt heat rushing under her skin. The great thing about the notes had been the anonymity, the freedom to say whatever she wanted without having to gauge his reaction. She wasn't sure she could read the highly personal words aloud.

His left hand cupped the side of her face, drawing her closer. Stevie's eyes drifted shut when their breath mingled the second before he claimed her. His parted lips were moist and firm as his mouth slanted over hers in a kiss that was both a slow exploration and a tantalizing challenge.

She followed the pace he set as she traced the contours of his mouth with her tongue. Then she sensed the hunger building inside him and released the reins on her own passion, eagerly ravishing his mouth as desire sang through her veins. Her heart raced and her body fairly vibrated with pent-up desire.

He gently stroked her cheeks with smooth, circular motions as he pulled back to look into her eyes. The invitation in his heated gaze was obvious, the silence ripe with expectancy. Then the musical notes of his cell phone broke the spell. His eyes darkened in annoyance but he kept his tone light.

"I'm sorry. That might be Alex."

She suppressed a sigh and tried to ignore the damp heat between her thighs as she hopped off of his lap. It had better be Alex, and not one of those *cariñas.* Whoever it was, they had lousy timing.

"As soon as I'm done, we can go into the other room and watch a movie...or something."

"I'll take the 'or something.'"

Emelio bent down to steal another quick kiss before retrieving his phone from the kitchen counter. "Sanchez."

"Hey, buddy. It's Jack Weston."

The hearty voice booming through the receiver made him wince. Maybe if he cut to the chase, the Assistant State's Attorney wouldn't talk his ear off for a change. "Jack. How's the Ramos trial going?"

No such luck. Weston began to relay the minute details of the court proceedings. The guy had goddamn lousy timing. Emelio stalked across the hallway to the office. He rocked back in his chair and stared out the window until he finally just interrupted.

"What can I do for you, Jack?"

"That's what I wanted to talk to you about. We might have to recall you to the stand."

Emelio set the front legs of the black-leather desk chair back on the floor. "What for? Alex and I already gave a week's worth of testimony."

Weston replied with a phony apologetic chuckle. "Hey, don't blame me. I'm just warning you about the possibility of bringing you back as a rebuttal witness."

Mierda. Emelio scrubbed one hand over his face. Since the judge hadn't excused him, he was technically still under oath and therefore obligated to appear before the court. That would leave Stevie in the hands of one of the agency's less experienced investigators if Alex was recalled as well.

Jack's too friendly voice broke into his thoughts. "Look, it may not even happen, but I've got to prep just in case. Why don't you swing by my office?"

"No can do. I'm out of town on an assignment." The cell phone trilled, signaling that the battery was dying. Emelio reached over to plug the charger into the wall.

"Well then, the next day. You'll be back from...?"

"I don't know if I'll be in Miami by then. This case could take a while."

Weston sighed in exasperation. "Where the hell are you?"

Emelio started to lose patience. If he were recalled to the stand, he'd deal with it. But right now Stevie was across the hall waiting for "something."

"Come on, Sanchez. Cut me some slack. We can't wait until the last minute to go over the court transcripts."

"I know, I know. But I can't reassign this one. How soon will you know for sure if you need me?"

"Soon." When he spoke, Weston's tone was several degrees cooler. "Depending on where you are, you can be here in a matter of hours, right? I guess I can give you about a day's notice."

"Great, Jack. Keep me posted."

Damn it. Emelio hoped his partner had caught that flight from Baltimore. Cursing under his breath, he put the cell phone on the charger and dialed Alex's number on the landline.

"Hey, partner. Are you back yet?"

"Almost. I'm just getting into a cab for home." He heard the sound of a door slamming, then Alex's voice giving directions to the driver. "Don't tell Meghan, but I'm really looking forward to an uninterrupted night. Whoever coined the phrase 'sleep like a baby' never lived with a newborn."

The quiet ache of jealousy surprised him. Alex had been lucky enough to find a terrific wife, and together they'd made an incredible little boy. While his best friend deserved every happiness, their friendship had naturally been altered and Emelio found himself longing for a family of his own.

He scraped the hair off his forehead. "Listen, Alex. I don't know how much time we have to figure out why Braga sent those photos, but it just got a lot shorter."

"Yeah? What's happened?"

"Weston called me tonight. Said they might have to recall us on rebuttal."

Alex's reaction was an immediate and ugly expletive. "You'd think two years on a case would be enough without having to deal with a monthlong trial, too.''

They rehashed the investigation and arrests, as well as speculating about Stevie's connection to Braga, until Emelio huffed out a breath and got to his feet. ''Okay. We can talk about the rest tomorrow. Right now I've got somebody waiting.''

There was silence on the other end of the phone, and then Alex growled in his ear. ''That had better not mean what I think, Em. Not after the hell you gave me for getting involved with Meghan when she was still a suspect.''

When they'd first arrived at the Cayo Sueño Resort hunting for Ramos and Braga, he'd had every reason to think that Meghan was working for the cartel, despite Alex's gut-level belief in her innocence. He knew Stevie couldn't be involved with Braga directly, but somehow she'd attracted his menacing attention. As for her innocence... The letters were proof against that.

''It doesn't mean anything, not yet.''

Alex scoffed. ''Bullshit.''

''What are you talking about?'' Emelio returned to the dining room, only to find it empty. The table had been cleared, the dishes removed and the candles blown out.

''Actually Meghan noticed before I caught on. Stevie's had her eyes on you for a while now, hombre. And you've done some looking of your own.''

No point in denying it—his best friend knew better. ''If I could ever get off the phone, I'd do more than just look.''

"Make sure you know what you're getting into this time."

Emelio dismissed his warning with a rude suggestion, appreciating Alex's concern but not the reference to what happened with his last relationship.

"See you, Em."

"Yeah, man. Later."

A fast check in the kitchen revealed clean countertops and a running dishwasher. But no Stevie. As he clicked off the cordless phone, he heard indistinct voices coming from the Florida room.

The brilliant color and dark shadow of several explosions flashed across Stevie's face. Her lithe body curled around a throw pillow on the white-leather sofa, her hands tucked under her cheek. She must have been tired to fall asleep before James Bond had escaped from the bad guys' lair and saved the world.

After lowering the volume on the entertainment center, Emelio covered her with the light blanket from one of the armchairs. Then he picked up the remote control and sat next to her. Impulsively, he reached down to lightly brush his fingers over the corn-silk strands of her hair. It seemed an oddly natural thing to do.

She stirred, instinctively seeking his touch. He'd never brought a woman to this house before. Even his family was rarely invited here and Alex had only stayed once. So why the hell did Stevie look so right, cuddled on the sofa beside him? Not in the mood to examine his actions, or the feelings behind them, Emelio settled in to watch Bond kick some Soviet ass.

5

EMELIO HAD FINALLY taken her to bed. Too bad he hadn't joined her for...anything.

Stevie sighed and rolled onto her right side, watching the morning sunlight glitter on the turquoise waters of the swimming pool. The muted whoosh of incoming waves on the Gulf was barely audible through the closed French doors as she snuggled under the hunter-and-burgundy satin quilt. Even Florida got chilly on January nights.

She wondered if she was lying on Emelio's side of the bed, and whether he slept on his back or his stomach. She wondered why he wasn't sleeping right beside her. Flopping over, she stared at the ceiling and worked on identifying her emotions, since she was already focused on the source.

Lust, pure and simple. She was definitely feeling lust. Her body hummed with an intense desire that had her aching for Emelio's touch. He was so right about the anticipation. Writing the black-lace letters had been fun, but now she wanted those erotic fantasies of making love with him to become real.

Then again, love wouldn't have anything to do with it.

Disappointment. As much as she hated to admit it, she was also feeling disappointed. Funny how she hadn't wanted more until he'd set a boundary on their time together. There was no way to look at Emelio and not want sex. But after seeing his paintings and discovering the passion below the surface of his professional veneer, she found that she wanted more.

Stevie pressed the edges of her palms against her eyes and sighed heavily. The stress of running from an unknown danger must have rendered her temporarily insane.

After divorcing Tom, she'd avoided men who seemed too demanding or controlling. Emelio had already proven he had no qualms about making decisions that affected her life, and yet she was still crazy about him. Or it could be she was just crazed with hunger. She'd never really finished dinner last night, as her stomach crankily reminded her.

She turned her left wrist and checked the hour. The Timex had been her father's. He taught her to tell time on that watch, she remembered. Then he'd made himself a fortune in commercial real estate and traded his old Timex for a flashy diamond Rolex. His jewelry wasn't the only thing that had changed....

Kicking off the covers with a scowl, she swung her legs over the bed. She assumed the Mountain Pose and she ran through a series of Yoga stretches, emptying her mind and warming up her body. When she'd finished her morning routine, she went to see about some food.

The cottage was quiet, only the tranquil sounds of the water and birdsong breaking the silence. Her bare feet padded across the carpeted floors onto the cool terra-cotta tiles as she wandered through the house. Eventually, she found Emelio asleep in the Florida room.

He didn't look too comfortable stretched out on the

sofa, his long coffee hair tousled and one arm flung over his head. Judging by the rumpled blanket tangled around his legs and hanging to the floor, he'd spent a restless night. Sunshine streaming through the glass walls highlighted the uneasy lines tightening his forehead.

It also gleamed off the stainless-steel barrel of a gun positioned within arm's reach on the floor. She didn't pick it up, but estimated it took a .45 caliber shell. Nine of them in fact. Emelio meant what he said about protecting her.

But why had he chosen to subject himself to the sofa when there was plenty of room in the king-size bed? Knowing him, he probably thought he was being considerate. Emelio had been so good to her in the last twenty-four hours, allowing her into his home and letting her discover his secrets. There had to be some way to show her appreciation.

Her belly gurgled again, offering a solution. An old adage proclaimed that the fastest way to a man's heart was through his stomach, so she'd wake him with a nice breakfast. But what should she make? She usually just poured herself a bowl of chocolate-frosted sugar bombs.

Beignets and café au lait—a little taste of New Orleans. She used to watch their cook make the square doughnuts for her as a girl, but she was pretty sure about the recipe. Draping the blanket back over him, she carefully leaned over to brush a soft kiss on Emelio's cheek. He murmured something in response then continued to sleep.

In the kitchen, Stevie quietly opened and closed all of the cabinets until she found a couple of mixing bowls and a frying pan. Once she located the main ingredients in the pantry, she dropped a package of active yeast and a bottle of cooking oil onto the island countertop.

Okay. She remembered this part. She stirred the dry yeast into some hot water, then turned on the stove burner and added a couple tablespoons of oil to the frying pan. That's as far as she got before running into a problem. Not being a gourmet cook, she wasn't prepared for the choices Emelio's pantry forced her to make.

Was she supposed to use all-purpose or self-rising flour for the beignets? She figured it was the self-rising since the donuts were supposed to be big and fluffy. But did she need Ten-X sugar or confectioner's? And what the hell was raw sugar?

Passing the stove, she noticed the oil was sizzling and reduced the heat under the burner. She dumped six cups of flour into the largest mixing bowl, raising a cloud of soft white dust in the process. Then she remembered she needed milk. But was it buttermilk or condensed milk?

Damn. This was why she ate cold cereal for breakfast.

She pulled the carton of eggs they'd bought yesterday out of the fridge and grabbed the regular whole milk since it was all they had. The first egg was ruined when she crushed the shell into jagged fragments and it dripped onto the countertop.

She'd only blended the first four cups of flour into the yeast when her arm started to get tired. Tossing the wooden spoon into the sink, she opened and closed more cabinets, looking for an electric mixer. She needed to hurry because she'd forgotten to add cinnamon to the thick batter.

"What the hell...?"

At the sound of his voice, Stevie dropped the mixer on her foot and yelped in pain. Turning, she saw Emelio stare in horror at the plume of black smoke unfurling from the burned oil. In two steps, he reached the stove and yanked the pan off the heat.

He started to say something then stopped when he looked past her shoulder at the island. His features took on a strange expression while he glanced from her to the counter and back. Color warmed his face, his mouth twisted in a funny way and his eyes had a glassy sheen.

"What's growing over there?"

"Oh, nooo!"

Stevie hobbled to the huge mess oozing out of the mixing bowl and onto the countertop. The batter had risen—and kept on rising—taking on a life of its own. Tears of frustration welled up in her eyes and she fought hard to keep them from spilling over while she filled the sink with hot water and dish soap.

"It was supposed to be beignets. I wanted to surprise you, but not like this. Don't worry. I'll clean everything up." She looked over at him and that's when it happened.

Amusement danced in his hazel eyes. A muscle quivered in his jaw and a little dimple appeared beside his mouth. His lips stretched until the corners turned up, slowly parting to reveal even white teeth. The grin continued to blossom on his face and then he burst into laughter.

Stevie's tears dried instantly as she stared at him in wonder. My God, Emelio was smiling. It was a dazzling sight, so genuine and so irresistible. She'd thought he was handsome before, but with that smile he was devastating. Her heart turned over, spreading warmth to her already hot cheeks.

Holding his sides, he gasped for breath. "When you said you'd do anything to make me smile, I didn't expect you to destroy my kitchen. It looks like a flour bomb went off."

Stevie twisted her lips into a grimace and scooped the batter into the trash. After shoving the mixing bowls into the hot water, she tossed the spatula in after them. The soapy splashes on her T-shirt only made him chuckle harder.

"I'm glad you think this is funny. We'll see how funny it is when you have to do all of the cooking from now on."

"Come here, Stevie." Emelio walked over to her side, still grinning. Taking one hand, he drew her into his arms and held her gaze as he slowly reached up. But instead of the caress she'd expected, he made a brushing motion. "You've got flour on your face."

Her shoulders sagged and she dropped her forehead onto his chest, shaking her head in defeat. "Not a good morning."

Emelio's warm fingers touched her chin, encouraging her to look up at him. The humor in his amber-green eyes had been replaced by something else, something more. His melodic voice held a deep emotion when he spoke.

"Thank you."

His mouth descended on hers in a kiss that was unexpectedly tender. His lips glided over hers like a whispered promise, giving and asking nothing in return. She drank in the sweetness of his kiss, and felt the warm glow of happiness spreading through her heart. He held her closer for a tight hug and then stepped back.

Emelio playfully planted a smooch on her nose before moving toward the refrigerator. "How about I fix us another breakfast."

She glanced up at the wisps of smoke still hanging in the air. "How about we get dressed and go out to eat?"

"That's not really a good idea." He pulled the eggs out again and chose a steak from the freezer.

Stevie's forehead furrowed. "Why not? We're perfectly safe here in Naples."

"Rule number one of 'real' investigative work. Never assume that you're safe anywhere." He set the food down and looked over at her. "I talked to Alex a few minutes ago. He sent Jason and Rick over to your apartment to investigate. There were several hang-ups on your answering machine and the building super said some guy was looking for you last night."

She closed her eyes briefly, clenching her stomach as she slowly exhaled.

"Somebody called the office this morning, too, asking to speak to either one of us. They refused to give Tiffnee a name or say what they wanted. Braga's sending people out to find us, Stevie, so we're not going to take any chances."

She curled her hand into a fist, her fingernails digging into the palm as the familiar anxiety skipped along her nerves. She couldn't stay locked up in the house. She couldn't. Stevie tried to hide her dread behind a show of bravado.

"You really think Braga is going to walk up to us at a sidewalk café? Maybe he'll jump out from behind a clothing rack in one of the shops."

He crossed his arms over his broad chest, an uncompromising look in his eyes. "I'm not willing to risk your life—"

"You said yourself that you never bring anyone here. You called this house 'José's place' so I assume it's in your other name. There's no way Braga could track us down. So don't tell me I can't go out!" She knew she was being unreasonable, but another part of her, the part she'd paid dearly to save, protested vehemently against the idea of confinement.

Emelio's tone became as carefully expressionless as his features. "I didn't say you couldn't go. I'm just strongly recommending against it."

"Don't do that." She spoke from between clenched jaws as resentment coiled inside her, escalating her temper from *annoyed* to *incensed.*

"I realize this is frustrating and you don't have any experience—"

"Don't goddamn do that!" It was happening again. Her life was being controlled again. She stared at him through hooded eyes, shaking with impotent rage. "I hate that overly logical condescending tone, like I'm some recalcitrant child."

Emelio remained where he stood, as if he thought a sudden approach would really set her off, and yet she sensed him reaching out to her. "Tell me what this is really about."

Verbalizing it would reveal how weak, how helpless and pathetic she used to be. In her nightmares, she still saw that house, the old rambling Victorian in Faubourg Marigny where she'd been trapped, suffocating in the confines of her fear. She had been too young, too damaged to know how to get free, certain that she deserved what she got.

She didn't want Emelio to know. Then again, maybe if she explained, he'd understand why she wouldn't tolerate taking orders or being restricted. Stevie pressed a hand against her stomach. "I couldn't go anywhere—I had to ask. Whenever I did go out, Tom had me followed...."

His hazel eyes softened in understanding, but she turned away from his pity. The last thing she wanted was pity.

"I'm sorry, Stevie. But I'm responsible for protecting you and your safety has to come first."

EMELIO'S VISION of a leisurely breakfast followed by a short walk along the beach had incinerated under Stevie's aggravated glare. Given her history, it was no wonder the idea of being constrained in any way set her off. But he had to think about what was best for her.

He leaned against the doorway of the home gym and watched Stevie attack a training bag hanging from the ceiling. A half hour had passed, but her temper hadn't subsided one bit. Even wearing gloves, her knuckles would be black-and-blue as hard as she was hitting the padded leather. No doubt she was imagining him in the bag's place.

He stroked his fingers lightly over the fading bruise on his chin. That woman had a mean left hook when she was angry. Her gray-blue eyes, turbulent as a gathering storm over the Gulf, briefly met his in the mirror. If looks could kill...

Stevie altered her stance and delivered several roundhouse kicks. Emelio winced in sympathy as the bag took a direct hit to the side of its "head." If he had been in its place, she would have decapitated him for sure.

As he continued to watch her, he experienced an intriguing blend of caution, respect and lust. She had changed into a zippered sport bra and spandex bike shorts that accentuated the firm curves of her bottom. The tight material left her arms and legs bare and left even less to his active imagination.

Like everything else she did, Stevie approached exercise with concentrated intensity. Her finely sculpted biceps and the lean muscles of her thighs strained as she worked off her frustration. He could hear her breathing, deep and ragged, as each powerful impact resounded against the padded leather. Her strength made her just a little dangerous and that danger was a complete turn-on.

A sheen of sweat glistened on her lightly tanned skin. Emelio's gaze followed a trickle of moisture as it rolled along her graceful neck and over her chest to disappear between her breasts. The low neckline of her sport bra drew his attention to the taut peaks of her nipples. He swallowed hard and shifted to ease the pressure inside his nylon pants, glad that the loose basketball jersey he wore ended below his waist.—

"Hey, champ. Why not give the training bag a break and take me on instead?"

She pivoted with a smirk, her eyes darting down the front of his body and back up to his face. She held his gaze for a second, and he could almost see the wheels turning in her mind. Then she unfastened her gloves and tossed them toward the weight bench behind her.

"The only place I'm taking you is down."

He bared his teeth in a grin that was beginning to

feel natural again, gladly accepting her challenge. If Stevie was looking to burn off some energy with a few hours of contact sports, he was willing to oblige. The air between them crackled with electricity born of equal parts antagonism and lust. They were both feeling edgy, making the spacious house feel way too small.

He pushed away from the doorframe and prowled toward her, deliberately infusing his words with innuendo. "Are you as good as you've led me to believe?"

She blinked twice at the double entendre, and then her plump lower lip curved into a Mona Lisa smile. She raked the tendrils of dark honey hair back from her forehead with both hands, a movement that thrust her chest forward.

"You have no idea how good I can be, chér."

"Not yet. But I know I'm better."

"Really?" She taunted him with an arched eyebrow and a whole lot of attitude. "Are you willing to bet on it?"

Emelio stopped mere inches in front of her, close enough to feel the heat radiating from her lithe body, close enough to breathe the unique scent of her damp skin. He cocked his head to one side, the epitome of all-male arrogance, pitching his voice low and intimate.

"What do I get when I win?"

Stevie's eyes flashed a brilliant blue, the storm having lifted to reveal competitive interest and carnal desire. She stepped forward so that her breasts lightly brushed his chest, tilting her head back to look up at him. Her husky answer was delivered in a sensual drawl ripe with promise.

"When *I* win, the prize is winner's choice. And the winner takes all."

God, what a woman. A band of tension throbbed in his groin. He wanted to be inside her more than he wanted his next breath. But for now, he simply wanted to enjoy her.

"Deal."

When she offered her hand to shake on it, he braced his back leg and yanked her off balance. Stevie threw out her other hand as if to catch herself, then suddenly wrapped her arm around his neck. The choke hold was playful but she was exerting enough pressure to force him over. Not that he minded having his face pressed against her breast one bit. It was soft and warm and his mouth was watering for a taste…

"So, Emelio. What were you saying about being better? And here I thought you'd be a worthy opp—"

Before she could finish her sentence, he'd hooked one elbow behind her knees and lifted her into his arms. Stevie gave a startled yelp and loosened her grip on his neck just before he dropped to the mat in a modified body slam.

Flat on her back with a dazed expression, her moist lips parted invitingly as she tried to catch her breath. Unable to resist, Emelio leaned over to steal a kiss. Her body felt solid beneath his, taut but softly padded in all of the right places. She was hot in all of the right places, too, when he slid one leg between hers.

He slanted his lips over her soft, sexy pout then thrust his tongue inside to plunder the velvety warmth of her mouth. He reveled in her surrender when she threaded her fingers through his hair to draw him closer. Shifting his weight from his arms to his knees, he broke away just long enough to yank the jersey over his head.

He gave her a teasing grin as he pitched the shirt aside. "Some Jayne Bond you are."

Stevie's eyes narrowed when he reached for her again, a hint of gray clouding their blue depths. With a lightning attack, she hit him with a quick jab to the solar plexus. When he clutched his middle and doubled over, she gave him a shove that rocked him back on his butt.

"Hoo yah!" She bounded to her feet, arms raised overhead like a prize-fighter. Then she started doing a little victory dance that involved a lot of sexy wriggling and hip shaking. "You go, girl."

Her triumph only lasted until he swept her legs out from under her and she smacked the mat again. With a sound that was half laughter and half growl, she scrambled up and lunged for him. Emelio put his hands on her waist and drew his knees in so that they rolled over sideways. Lying on top of her, he watched Stevie's pupils dilate, saw the flash of desire in reaction to their compromising position.

At the same time, he was achingly aware of her breasts flattened against his bare chest, his erection pressing the apex of her thighs. He felt her heart pounding and the quick gasp of breath on his cheek. A combination of adrenaline and pheromones surged through him, hot and urgent. *Dios mio,* was it possible to take her right through their clothing?

Stevie wrapped her thighs around his waist, locking her ankles behind his back. If he got any harder, he'd split his pants. Then she torqued her body until they rolled over again and she ended up on top, straddling his lap. When he struggled, she clamped her thighs tighter until he lay still.

"I win, chér." She gave him a saucy wink.

His voice was little more than a husky whisper. "Winner takes all. So take all of me."

In the space of a heartbeat, she captured his mouth in a kiss that seared his lips. A moan escaped her throat as their tongues met and mated. She kissed him deeply, desperately, wordlessly expressing how much she wanted him. The way she arched her back and wiggled on his lap drove him nuts.

Emelio slid his hands along her waist, felt the satin texture of her skin, felt her quiver at his touch. He reached between them to unzip the bra top, freeing her for exploration. Without breaking the kiss, Stevie managed to slip her arms out of the garment. Then she sighed against his mouth as he cupped the weight of her perfect breasts in his palms.

He brushed his thumbs over her nipples until they beaded into sensitive pebbles. Then he rose up to take one into his mouth. The flick of his tongue on the engorged flesh made her quiver, gasp and press closer as he suckled each breast in turn. Stevie cradled his head in order to capture his mouth for another kiss. Her bare torso molded to his chest and he let his palms glide over the lean muscles and smooth skin.

He pushed his fingers beneath the elastic band of her shorts so he could explore the contours of her backside. Alternately rubbing and squeezing the pliant flesh, he flexed his hips, circling his arousal between her thighs. Her tongue darted in and out and around his mouth, urging him to a faster rhythm. Her skin was hot beneath his hands and the squirming became frantic.

Stevie was on the verge of coming but damned if she was going over the edge without him. "I've got to have you, lady. But I need to get something first."

She reluctantly pushed back on her heels. Breathing hard, her face flushed with color, he saw that her eyes were slightly glazed and the irises had darkened to cobalt. He felt a Neanderthal surge of pride knowing that his woman wanted him as badly as he craved her. With one hand on his knee for leverage, Emelio got up to strip and find some condoms.

When he returned, Stevie was undressed and stood waiting for him. Her body was extraordinary, beautifully proportioned from her strong shoulders to her sculpted torso, slender waist and gently rounded hips. His gaze lingered on her breasts, watched the rush of heat beneath the skin, darkening her nipples to a rosy brown. He noticed the lack of swimsuit lines on her sun-toasted skin and smiled. She kept on surprising him.

A blur of color caught his attention in the mirror and he narrowed his eyes to bring it into focus. The small purple butterfly tattoo hovered at the base of her spine, its delicate wings spread gracefully just above that gorgeous butt. He hadn't thought it was possible to get any more turned on, but the sight of her body art was incredibly sexy.

In less than five seconds they were back in each other's arms. As his tongue teased her mouth open, she deepened the kiss. Her lips angled across his over and over until his breath came in harsh gasps. She kissed him wildly, frantically, while grinding her pelvis against him.

The silken hairs covering her mound rasped against his rigid flesh, bringing him to the edge of his control.

Then she reached one hand between their bodies to grasp his penis. He let out a frustrated groan as she stroked him with firm but gentle fingers. He couldn't wait another second—he had to have her or he would explode.

Heart thundering in his chest, Emelio bent his knees slightly and gripped the back of Stevie's thighs. He lifted her up, supporting her weight with his hands. She draped her arms over his shoulders when he started to carry her across the room. "Hang on to me, lady. I'm going to make your fantasy from black-lace letter number four come true."

6

STEVIE GASPED when she felt the cool mirror against her back, but it quickly warmed from the heat of her body. Emelio claimed her open mouth, tempting and teasing, building the excitement. His kiss thrilled her, aroused her. Finally being naked in his arms was better than she'd ever imagined. He'd offered to make her fantasies come true, but he was creating another one even now.

She chased his tongue while his firm, full lips slid expertly across hers. She stroked her fingers over the golden-brown skin on his shoulders, along the rock-solid triceps that bunched with the effort of holding her aloft. Emelio's hands, the hands she'd dreamed of for months, felt smooth and strong and secure as he tightened his grip on her thighs.

Her nipples grazed the crisp hairs on his chest before her breasts flattened against the hard planes. She could feel the ridges of his sculpted abs against her belly. A knot of tension, the best kind of tension, formed in her feminine core and made her tingle everywhere their bodies merged.

Stevie inhaled the heady scent of citrus, sweat and male as she pressed her mouth to the strong pulse thudding in his neck. When her lips brushed the tender spot behind his ear, he jolted. A low chuckle escaped her even as he moaned softly in delight.

It seemed Mr. Calm, Cool and Controlled came undone with the right touch in the right places.

Emelio repositioned himself within her widespread thighs. He moved forward so that the smooth tip of his penis was poised at her entrance. She tried to relax, to prepare for the sensual invasion, but she was too eager, too needy.

Raising her eyes to his face, she saw that he was struggling to keep still. Fire lit his hazel eyes, changing their color to a deep bronze, as he met her stare. That molten expression left no doubt that he wanted her, that he had every intention of taking her.

And yet he remained motionless. Her eyebrows wrinkled in confusion. She'd been waiting so long, thinking and fantasizing about him, needing him. She was desperate to have him inside her, crazy with unbridled lust. But for some reason he held back....

Understanding slowly dawned. Somehow Emelio had sensed the vulnerability beneath her desire, and he was waiting for her permission. Even now, with his erection straining against her and sweat beading on his golden skin, he considered her feelings. Something dark and tightly closed within her shattered and she fought the sudden urge to cry.

If she didn't already have feelings for Emelio, she would have fallen in love with him then and there. The warmth permeating her heart spread through her body until the flames of desire ignited again. Wrapping her legs more securely around his waist, her hoarse words were both a plea and a command.

"Take me."

She clung to him while he guided his penis into the slick wetness of her passage. He slowly lowered her onto his shaft, inch by magnificent inch, until his sex was completely sheathed in hers. Her vaginal muscles contracted around his unfamiliar thickness, trying to draw him deeper still. She writhed in pleasure as her body softened and stretched to accept him.

Emelio pushed into her once, withdrew slightly, and then returned. Stevie gasped. It had been so long. She moved to the rhythm of his thrusts, moaning loudly when she felt the quickening in her womb. The delicate inner shivers rippled through her and her body wept with the force of her climax.

"Again, lady. I want to feel that again."

His muscular arms cradled her body while he shifted her against the wall. Panting hoarsely, he set the slow, sensuous pace. Each time he lifted and lowered her, his powerful body elicited a deep, persistent throbbing inside her.

Stevie squeezed his waist with her thighs, encouraging him to increase the tempo. Instead of satisfying her, that first orgasm had left her wanting more. But he continued to slide into her and draw back out at a deliberate pace, his groans muffled against her shoulder.

"Please, chér. I need—"

"No, not yet. It feels too damned good."

She was desperate for the second climax that was hotly coiled inside her, but Emelio kept it just beyond her reach and for once she didn't resent a man's taking control. She relaxed and gave herself over to the steady rhythmic friction. Angling her head to rest against his neck, she nibbled a path to his collarbone, delighting in his reaction.

Each tiny bite caused him to shudder and flex. The sounds he uttered were a blend of laughter and moaning. She was thrilled to know she made him as wild as he drove her. He rocked his hips faster, heightening the pleasure until they were both frantic for release. Finally, gloriously, his body convulsed inside her; her body trembled around his.

Stevie went limp in his arms, the harsh sound of his breath fanning her ear. Emelio held on to her but his whole body was shaking. Only his strength kept them from collapsing in a heap onto the padded mats. He rested his forehead against the mirror, exhausted, spent and squishing her. With a groan, she unlocked her legs and slid down until her feet touched the floor.

He stood with his eyes closed and his hands resting on her hips, his body still quivering. She was pretty shaky herself. Even though he'd done all of the work, she felt as weak as a kitten after that series of incredible orgasms. Stevie planted a kiss on his jaw, lowered her arms from his neck and squeezed out from between him and the wall.

His grasp on her fingers halted her in place. "Where do you think you're going? We're not done."

She answered him with a husky laugh, surprised that she was ready for him again so soon. "I didn't think we were. But you only brought one condom."

"Hmm, good point. I'll be right back."

While he went to get them some protection, Stevie took the opportunity to go into the guest bathroom and clean up a little. On the way out, she heard the distinctive chime of his cell phone. She glanced down the hall but didn't see him.

"Emelio? Hey, Emelio?"

When he didn't reply, she hesitated for a second, but then figured she'd already opened his mail. It might be Alex calling with information. Stevie located the cell phone in Emelio's office and depressed the answer button.

"Sanchez, um, residence."

"Hello?"

A sultry female voice with a slight accent had replied. The caller wasn't Alex. It was one of the *cariñas.* Suddenly feeling very territorial, Stevie let her voice slide into a cool, unfriendly tone. "Can I help you?"

"I'm trying to reach Emelio, but I must have dialed the wrong number...."

"You've got the right number."

"This is Maggie." Matching attitude for attitude, her voice became sharply demanding. "Who are you?"

The woman who intends to replace you. Her mouth twisted into a frown but she spoke in a sweetly cooperative manner. "Sorry, Maggie. Emelio's a little naked right now. How about I take a message or have him call you when I'm finished with him?"

The answering wail was high-pitched and loud enough to pierce Stevie's eardrum. She hung up the cell phone in midscreech and turned to find Emelio standing behind her. His dark hair had been combed away from his forehead and he smelled faintly of soap. She allowed her gaze to drift lower.

Wow. As attractive as he was dressed, his bare body was a gorgeous sight to behold. She hadn't gotten a good look before he'd taken her against the wall. His body was perfect—long and sinewy and wonderfully proportioned.

His wide shoulders emphasized his broad chest, muscular arms and lean torso. A dusting of hair fanned across his chest before converging to form a path that led down his stomach and disappeared into the thatch around his loins. Desire, hot and greedy, danced in her veins.

"Who called?"

The carefully controlled tone of his voice drew her attention back to his face. "Um, somebody named Maggie…"

That brooding expression stole back onto his features. Maybe she should have let his voice mail pick up after all. Emelio spoke from between gritted teeth, his hazel eyes hooded in exasperation.

"Do you have *any* idea what you've just done?"

Guilt made her defensive and so the apology that had been on the tip of her tongue melted like a snowflake. She propped one fist on her naked hip and glared right back. "Yeah, I got rid of one-third of my competition."

Emelio quirked one eyebrow at her bold declaration and she saw some of the annoyance recede from his gaze. He crossed his arms over the expanse of his chest and tilted his head to one side. "Nooo. You just ruined my life."

Could he be any more dramatic? Her temper leaped right into *seriously pissed off.* They had just experienced the absolute best sex of her entire life. She could still feel the imprint of his body all over hers. But had it meant anything to him? Nooo. He was all bent out of shape over his goddamn *cariña.* She threw the phone at him, grudgingly impressed by his swift reflexes when he caught it in one hand.

"Okay, I realize it wasn't the most adult thing I've done lately. But all I did was tell your girlfriend—excuse me, one of your girlfriends, that we had sex. I don't know how you find the time to juggle three of them anyway. Maybe you should thank me for lightening your social calendar."

His eyebrows slammed together. "Thank you?!"

Stevie scowled right back. "You're welcome."

"Smart ass." He brushed by her to toss his cell phone on the desk, shaking his head and muttering in Spanish.

What in the world was wrong with her? Stevie knew she'd acted like a possessive witch, but she couldn't help it. She felt so resentful that she didn't have all of his attention and he'd made her so damn mad... She turned to face him, one fist planted on her hip while the other hand punctuated her words.

"Listen, I don't share or play well with others. So when I heard her voice, I went with an impulse and—"

"And just ratted me out to my sister Magdalena."

She startled, blinking in surprise. His sister? Her mind went blank as she tried to process this new information.

"Maggie won't so much as take a breath before she tells my other two sisters, Consuela and Angelina. Then, all three of them will break the land speed record to inform my very old-fashioned, very Catholic mother that, despite me lecturing the girls about abstinence, I'm having sex outside of marriage."

Stevie felt the hot flush of her mistake spread to both sets of cheeks. Connie, Angie and Maggie, the three *cariñas,* were his sisters.

"Oh."

"That's all you have to say?"

"Um."

Emelio crossed his arms over his chest and regarded her through hooded eyes. "You're getting more eloquent by the second, lady. Don't answer my phone again."

Her pulse stilled for an instant as she realized the significance of what she'd done. She'd been unforgivably rude to Maggie. She had embarrassed Emelio, made him look like a hypocrite in his family's eyes. And yet, he hadn't so much as raised his voice to her.

She'd never behaved like this before, had never been *allowed* to, not by her parents and sure as hell not by her ex-husband. That she instinctively knew it was safe to express her emotions around Emelio said more about the depth of her feelings than she wanted to deal with at the moment.

"I'm really sorry."

"I'd better call home later. Much later. *Gracias a Dios,* we're on the other side of the state."

Stevie ducked her chin and peered at him from beneath her lashes, wondering what degree burn she'd get from this level of embarrassment. At the same time, though, she was filled with a sense of jubilant relief.

"So, those woman who always call you at the office. Those calls were from your sisters, not your girlfriends?"

"That's right. I'm not involved with anyone else—Wait." Emelio broke off in midsentence with a little thrill of surprise and amusement. Stevie was jealous. Warmth spread through him as his lips curved into a smile. "You actually thought I was dating three different women at the same time?"

Flustered, she twisted her fingers. "Well, yeah. I mean, that's why I started writing the black-lace letters in the first place. I figured that was the only way to get your attention."

She already had it, though he'd tried to deny it. He pinched her chin between his thumb and index finger, tilting it up until she met his gaze. "I'm not seeing anyone right now, Stevie. You don't have to be jealous. So don't attack the next woman who calls me, please."

"I really am sorry about that." She reached over and wrapped her arms about his waist. "Would you like me to talk to your sisters and—"

"No!"

Stevie tightened her grip on his waist and rocked from side to side, creating a delicious friction everywhere their bodies touched. She offered him an innocently contrite look that was completely at odds with the seductive sway of her hips. "There must be some way I can make this up to you."

He responded with a slow grin as he ran his palms along the curve of her hips. "I think I can come *up* with some ideas."

"Didn't you say something about getting more condoms?"

"They're on the bed. We should probably go join them."

Emelio bent down and caught hold of the backs of Stevie's knees. He stood upright and carried her toward the bedroom in a modified fireman's lift.

"Hey!" She squealed and twisted around in protest of his caveman technique, then swatted him on the ass when he refused to let go of her. In the bedroom, he laid her down on the sheets amid a handful of brightly colored foil packets before following her onto the bed.

"Now, about how you can make things up to me."

Stevie reached under her back and pulled out a condom. "Just how many of these things did you get?"

"Enough to show you that you don't have any competition."

Two condoms and a catnap later, Emelio lazily trailed his fingers up and down her shoulder. She purred with contentment and shifted deeper into his arms. He sighed lightly, savoring the moment, all of his reasons for not getting involved with her forgotten. He could very happily remain in bed, holding her close, but he sensed her restlessness.

"What do you want to do with the rest of our afternoon?"

Stevie raised her head to look at him, eyes shining. Judging from her animated expression and bright smile, he figured he was in for another round of fantasy sex. *Dios mio,* he'd better take some vitamin supplements if he was going to keep up with her.

"There's something I've been dying to try. It seems easy, but I'm betting it's more complicated than it looks."

He didn't think the chandelier in the dining room was strong enough to hold their weight. For her, though, he was willing to try anything. "What's that, Stevie?"

"I want you to teach me how to hot-wire the Jeep."

"YOU LEARN FAST." Emelio followed Stevie into the kitchen. He grabbed a couple of glasses from the cabinet while she got the orange juice.

Since the Jeep had a manual transmission, he'd shown her how to pop start the ignition by rolling it down an incline and then snapping the clutch, as well as how to use the wires. Stevie successfully started the engine both ways several times. After that, she'd wanted to sneak over to the neighbors and practice on a different kind of vehicle.

Instead, he'd found a way to redirect her relentless enthusiasm. He should have known better than to challenge her to bypass the cottage alarm system. "Remind me to call Martin Security about those upgrades. Damn good thing I've got a backup alarm system for the art studio. I can't believe you disabled the motion sensors."

"It's a matter of knowing how the alarm circuit works and then choosing the right wires, just like with the Jeep." Stevie cracked some ice into the glasses and poured the juice. She grinned, but kept her tone light and modest. "Besides, I've got pretty good hand-eye coordination."

"Yes, you do." He gave his voice a suggestive inflection. The afternoon's activities had included casual brushes of a finger along a wrist, "accidental" bumps of a hip against a backside and quick kisses to any available patch of bare skin. "Still, I've got a business-grade system. I thought it would be harder to circumvent."

"Oh, it will be for your average B and E guy, but it's still a very good system. I'm just better. For one of my classes, I had an instructor who was an expert vault technician—"

Emelio arched one eyebrow in response to something in her tone. "Is that by any chance a euphemism for safecracker?"

Stevie chuckled. "How did you guess? He's reformed, though. Anyway, you can't design secure systems without knowing exactly where the weaknesses are and how to counteract them." She drank half of her juice while he reached into the fridge for sandwich fixings.

"I'm curious. How did you get into all of these...unusual training courses?"

"That's classified information. If I told you, I'd have to kiss you within fifteen seconds to keep from self-destructing."

Emelio leaned over to seal his mouth to hers, enjoying the tang of orange on her lips. He slid his tongue inside, indulging in a slow, hot exploration. When he dragged his mouth away, he saw that the kiss had left her glassy-eyed and breathless. He smiled.

"Wouldn't want you to self-destruct."

"Always looking out for my safety, aren't you?" She pretended to fan herself as she drained her glass.

He spread mustard on the bread slices and began layering the deli meat on top. "So, you were telling me about your secret-agent education."

"Oh, yeah. When I first came to Miami, one of the first things I did was sign up for a self-defense class. That's where I met Bernie. He taught Effective Defense for Women at the fitness center, but he also runs a bodyguard training academy. I did really well in his Tactical Weapons Proficiency course."

"Weapons Proficiency." Emelio leaned his back against the counter and crossed his arms. He was beginning to suspect that Stevie didn't just go after what she wanted, she hunted it down and jumped on it. "You're serious about wanting to be a field investigator, aren't you?"

"Yes, Emelio, I am." She planted her hands on her hips. "I started off learning for my own safety, then it became kind of a hobby. I realize most of the stuff I've learned was just for fun. But I want to do more than install alarms and cameras."

He gave a dry laugh. "It sounds like you're already qualified to invade a small country single-handedly. But you still need criminology and legal classes, investigative training—"

"The State of Florida doesn't require that for licensing—"

"But our agency requires it for hiring, along with some practical experience." When she opened her mouth to keep arguing, he raised a hand to interrupt her. "Let's deal with this after things settle down, okay?"

Stevie angled her head and frowned, but then conceded the point. "Just know, I intend to get my way on this one."

"That should probably scare me. In the meantime, I've got some business to take care of in the office." After cleaning up the kitchen, he carried the sandwiches across the hall and indicated Stevie should sit at the desk. "Real investigative work is mostly phone calls and fact checking."

She settled onto the black-leather chair and looked up at him. "What do you need me to do?"

Emelio leaned over to switch on his laptop computer. "Use the remote access dial-up to get into your computer files at the agency while I make some calls."

"We can do both at the same time?"

"Yeah, I've got a dedicated digital subscriber line."

"Cool." She connected to the Internet and finally

to the agency network server. ''Which files are you interested in?''

''All of them.'' She swung her head to stare at him. ''I know, I know. But I warned you about the fact checking. Can you skim through any case that has your name flagged as either primary or assist? See if anything jogs your memory.''

''All of them, huh?'' Stevie sighed heavily, then rolled her shoulders and ran her fingers across the keyboard, calling up her computer files. ''When do we get to the fun stuff, like chasing bad guys and shooting people?''

''Sorry, Jayne. You've been watching too much television again. But I'll see if I can round up some Communist extremists for you.''

He gave her a quick kiss on the nape of her neck, then grabbed the cordless phone and his sandwich, settling into the armchair by the window.

In between bites of salami and provolone on rye, he coordinated his investigation efforts with Alex. Although they'd worked together for three years in the Special Operations Division, they had different sources and contacts. Being away from Miami made it tough to get hold of his usual informants, so he tried calling some former colleagues.

David Heintz at the Bureau's North Miami Beach field office had taken over the Ramos case when Emelio left to join January Investigations. ''Braga? He's been quiet. Real quiet.''

''Have you got people watching him?''

''Closer than ever, what with the trial. But Braga hasn't so much as spit on the sidewalk.''

Emelio thanked him, and then gave Oscar Solis over at the DEA a ring. ''We've got nothing, Sanchez. The man is laying so low he's not casting a shadow.''

A half-dozen calls later, he banged the phone on the table in frustration. Stevie swung around in the chair to face him. ''You're not having much luck, either, huh. Why not? Based on the photo outside of my bank, he's obviously right in Miami.''

Emelio leaned back and crossed one ankle over the opposite knee. ''Braga's cunning, and very, very careful. Knowing he's a ruthless son of a bitch and getting a conviction are two different things.''

''Why didn't he go to jail after the Overtown shooting?''

''Politics. At that time, we didn't realize how big a fish Braga was. The SOD wanted to use him as bait to catch Ramos. Then, while we were on the case at Cayo Sueño, Braga all but told Alex he was staging a takeover. That's why Ramos is in protective custody until after he testifies.''

''You think Braga would actually try something?''

Emelio shrugged. ''Ramos chose to turn State's evidence rather than trust the man not to stab him in the back, literally.''

''This is driving me crazy, you know?'' Stevie dragged a hand through her hair. ''I have no idea what this man wants. And why me? It would make more sense for him to go after you and Alex.''

''We don't know for certain he's not.'' He laced his fingers over his stomach. ''That's why I've got people watching over my parents and sisters. Family means nothing to Braga.''

Stevie pushed back from the desk and paced the room. ''What about Alex? Aren't he and Meghan in danger, too?''

"As strange as this may sound, they probably aren't. Alex saved his life that night in Overtown and that may be reason enough for Braga to let him alone."

She stopped near the window and cocked her head to one side. "I don't get it. Alex was working the SOD case against Ramos. He went undercover to gather evidence and then testified at the trial, just like you did."

"Yeah, but Braga has a strange code of principles, a twisted kind of morality. He's fond of saying that he never forgets either a favor or a slight. Alex did him a favor."

"What did you do?"

Emelio curled his lips into a derisive smile. "Me? Not much. Just infiltrated the cartel and recruited an informant from Braga's own household."

Stevie lifted one eyebrow. "Oh. Is that all?"

"As far as Braga's concerned, that's more than enough."

7

AFTER A THURSDAY MORNING spent sleeping in, Emelio had cooked brunch, taken Stevie for that walk along the beach and watched two romantic-comedy videos with her. But now she was pacing the tiled floor in the Florida room, edgy and bored.

Emelio sat on the white-leather couch and watched her, amazed that one body could contain so much restless energy. Even in her sleep, Stevie tossed and turned, unable to keep still. "I have to make a phone call. After that, I'll see what else I can come up with to keep you entertained."

"That sounds promising."

Stevie turned from the glass wall and walked over to him. She leaned down to skim a kiss over his mouth, but the lighthearted gesture changed into something much more when she slipped her tongue between his lips. The kiss was hard and hot and hungry. After a fraction of a second, so was he.

"Don't take too long, chér."

A low purr of pleasure escaped him as she nuzzled his neck. He stroked his fingers along her thigh in return. When she moved back, he cleared his throat and shifted on the couch to adjust the throbbing erection she'd inspired. Then he picked up the phone and dialed home.

As he waited through the ringing, he watched

Stevie through lust-hooded eyes as she stood up to unzip her short rose-colored skirt. He reached out a hand to stroke her bare thigh. Then she slowly turned around, wriggling the skirt down her shapely hips, and offered him a damn fine view of the purple-and-black butterfly tattoo before dropping the garment to the floor.

"Bueno."

"Es Emelio. Cómo esté usted?"

"I want to talk with...her."

His mother was calm, but it was the kind of calm that had preceded a storm of lectures in rapid-fire Spanish when he was growing up. He could just imagine what a scandal Maggie's gossip had created. "Um, I don't think—"

"You are ashamed of her, no? This is why you never say nothing about this woman?"

"That's not true."

He was finding it difficult to focus now that Stevie had stripped off the pale pink knit top as well. She wasn't wearing a bra and the nipples of her perfect breasts hardened to mouthwatering peaks. His eyes roamed over her finely sculpted body in blatant appreciation.

"Emilio?"

"It's complicated. She's working for me and—"

"You are paying her?" His mother's voice rose in horror.

Emelio snapped his attention back to the conversation. "Yes. I mean, no! She's an investigator at the agency."

Stevie froze in the middle of a grind-wiggle-shimmy, obviously guessing that she was the topic of conversation. She picked up her top, covering her breasts, and waited.

"Well, why is she not at the agency? Why is she saying to your sister that you are naked?"

Emelio winced and closed his eyes. "That was a, um, misunderstanding. I'm on a case—"

"Hmph. Some case." There was a slight pause and he swore he could feel his mother trying to get inside his head, just like she'd done when he came home after curfew. "Emelio José, you are hiding something. Magdalena told Angelina—"

"Maggie exaggerated, I'm sure."

"Then let me talk to her, *mi hijo.* Since you have nothing to hide from your *familiá.*"

His mother's tone brooked no argument and, when she used that particular voice, it was easier to do as she ordered. He sighed and held up the receiver in his outstretched hand.

"It's for you."

"For me?"

Stevie narrowed her eyes at Emelio, her stomach suddenly quivering with dread. She didn't like that guilty expression he wore one single bit.

"Who is it?"

"My mother."

She shrank away from the telephone as though it would attack her. "You've got to be kidding. I don't want to—"

Emelio thrust the phone next to her face then raised both palms and sat back out of reach. Stevie shot him a withering look, then gulped in a draft of air.

"Hello, Mrs. Sanchez."

"So. You are having sexual relations with my son."

There was no sense in denying it, but she was in enough trouble with his family. Better to keep quiet now, and later, she'd make sure Emelio paid for this.

"I know nothing about you. Are you a nice girl? What kind of family do you come from? Do you go to church? I should at least know something about you before the wedding, no?"

"Wed— What?"

Stevie began to hyperventilate. Fortunately, Mrs. Sanchez continued speaking, saving her from having to reply.

"We have a lot to talk about, you and I. You tell my son to bring you home for dinner so that he can introduce you properly. And make sure you have clothes on."

Embarrassment had her cheeks flaming hot, as though Mrs. Sanchez could somehow tell she was only wearing pink cotton panties. "Yes, ma'am. I'll, uh, look forward to it."

"Hmph." Mrs. Sanchez hung up without another word.

Stevie rammed the phone back onto the cradle and glared at Emelio. "I cannot believe you did that!"

He tried unsuccessfully to plaster a contrite expression on his face, but the twinkle of amusement in his hazel eyes gave him away. "I'm very close to my family. You'll probably meet her sooner or later."

"I would have opted for much later, thank you."

He caught her wrist and gently pulled her into his arms. Ducking his head, he nuzzled her temple. "I'll make it up to you, Stevie. I promise."

"Damn right you will, chér. I want black-lace letter number five and I want it now."

Emelio felt his pulse leap at the gleam in Stevie's

eyes. *I dream of you, bound by my desire, a slave to my passion. I dream of you, hard and hot and helpless, as I urge you to the heights of ecstasy…* His body remembered that particular note as well as his mind did. Gravity doubled at the very thought of being restrained for Stevie's enjoyment.

"Five has always been my favorite number."

Holding her hand as they walked down the hallway in the direction of the master bedroom, he sensed her arousal by the fine tremor of her fingers. At the foot of the bed, he tried to take her into his arms again but she resisted.

"Strip. Then go lay down."

Stevie delivered the words like a command, but the effect was lost in the rough silk of her tone and the mischievous smile on her lips. It seemed that being in charge turned her on tremendously. Her gray-blue eyes sparkled like sunlight on water and her face was aglow with excitement.

Feeling pretty damn excited himself, Emelio pulled off the satin comforter. He threw several pillows to the floor then propped the remaining one upright. Settling on the smooth cotton sheets, he watched her peel off her panties. Anticipating that she'd join him, he made room for her on the bed.

His forehead furrowed in confusion when she darted for the walk-in closet instead. Stevie came back out a moment later with a fistful of his silk neckties.

"Are you okay with this?"

"I'm all yours, lady."

Her face lit up with a delighted expression. When she reached the side of the bed, she raised one arm over his head, indicating he should hold it aloft. His pulse thudded as she braced one knee beside him and leaned over to swiftly bind his wrist to the carved mahogany headboard.

Emelio arched forward to capture her right breast in his mouth. He traced circles around her flesh with his tongue and suckled her nipple to a hardened peak. He chuckled darkly. It was taking Stevie a lot longer to tie his other wrist.

"Now I've got you exactly where I want you." She sat back on her heels with a satisfied grin, the look on her face one of pure desire.

"What are you going to do with me?"

"Everything."

The feel of her warm hands trailing over his skin made him shiver. Certain areas like his neck had always been hyperresponsive but, with Stevie, the sensitivity of his entire body was heightened by her touch. "Everything" was probably going to kill him.

When he tried to wriggle away from the sensual torture, the slight pressure on his wrists reminded him of the situation. Silk tended to be slippery, though, so he could get loose anytime. He tugged his arms gently, testing the strength of the knots, only to discover they wouldn't give. Frowning slightly, he tugged a bit harder. Damn. Even though they were playing, he really was securely bound.

Stevie laughed at his efforts. "You're not going anywhere, chér. I got top grades in my Boating and Maritime Endurance courses. Those are bowlines with a half hitch, guaranteed not to slip under strain."

Maritime Endurance. Emelio knew a second of apprehension, not at all used to being at someone else's mercy. All his life, he'd been a leader, a decision maker. He'd been in charge. Now, he had to voluntarily submit to another's will, and he wasn't too sure he liked it. He flexed his hands, inwardly squirming. Game or no game, the lack of freedom made him damn uncomfortable.

Then he looked at Stevie, saw the twinkle in her eyes…and something else. Something he wasn't ready to acknowledge. But he knew without a doubt he was safe with her. He'd been dictating all of her decisions for the past three days. He could let her take control and have her revenge.

"You're all tied up and helpless… I can touch you any way and anywhere, and you can't stop me."

She stroked her fingers lightly up and down his chest, a look of triumph on her face. He closed his eyes briefly, lost in the sensations her touch elicited. His voice was hoarse when he finally replied. "I'm not complaining."

Stevie got to her knees, swung one leg over him to straddle his waist and settled her gorgeous ass on his lap. He breathed in the musky scent of her desire as he felt the dewy soft folds of her labia against the head of his penis. This was rapidly becoming his favorite position.

Stevie bent forward to trace the edges of his mouth with her tongue. He parted his lips, inviting her to go deeper, but she seemed content to slide her mouth slowly across his. He gently nibbled on her plump lower lip until she finally thrust her tongue forward and explored his mouth.

She shifted on top of him, brushing her mouth over his neck, making him quake as desire burned along his nerve endings. Then she bent over to suckle his left nipple. The wet tugging sensation sent a bolt of lust right to his groin.

His inability to move, to touch her in return, was both frustrating and exhilarating. Restricted as he was, his focus narrowed to the places where their bodies made contact. He felt the heat of her skin against his, the rasp of her pebbled nipples on his chest and the rough silk of her pubic hair brushing his thigh.

Her tongue blazed a hot, wet trail from his chest, along his abdomen and down to his groin. She eased lower, nipping his belly, licking his thigh and finally darting her tongue over his testicles. He dragged in a breath, gasping at the shock of that wickedly intimate kiss.

"I want you to watch me pleasure you, and know that you're powerless to do anything but lie back and enjoy it."

"No problem, as long as you never stop what you're doing."

She opened her mouth and took him between her soft, moist lips. The sensation of her tongue circling the head of his penis was almost his undoing. He had to grit his teeth to keep from shouting out loud as she nibbled and licked and sucked him to the brink of coming.

He closed his eyes, adrift in the gratification. She continued to slide her mouth up and down his shaft, her teeth lightly grazing his vulnerable flesh. Desire overwhelmed him in a powerful rush of heat and the tide of lust was rising fast. He was rock hard and on the verge of losing control.

It was going too fast, she made him feel too good. The sensation of her hot, talented mouth was beyond incredible, and he craved the sweet release that beckoned. But he didn't want their encounter to end too quickly. Hell, he didn't want it to end at all. And just when he knew he couldn't take anymore, she stopped.

"What—? Wait..."

"Just a second, chér. You're not dressed for this party."

Grabbing one of the foil packets, she opened it then tossed the wrapper aside. Stevie rolled a condom onto his rigid flesh and then crawled up his body until she settled on his lap once more. Moaning softly, she rubbed herself along his length, intensifying the pleasure by prolonging their satisfaction.

A slow ragged sigh escaped her throat as she sank down onto his rigid shaft. Arching her back, she braced both hands on his calves, changing the angle of penetration and increasing the glorious grinding pressure. She tossed her head and laughed, reveling in his hard, fast thrusts.

She looked wild and wanton, like a conquering Amazon, a warrior goddess whose lust was fueled as much by power as by desire. Stevie approached sex with the same persistent zeal she did everything else. He lay beneath her, sweat drenched and grinning and crazy about her.

But even as the long-denied emotions crept into his mind, he swiftly pushed them aside to be dealt with later. For now, he simply enjoyed her uninhibited use of his body.

Stevie reached down between them to massage the tiny bud of nerves at the core of her need. She rocked her pelvis back and forth to increase the friction until he couldn't distinguish his moans from hers. With a harsh cry, she continued to ride him and he rode the storm of mind-blowing sensation as she came hard, and then came again.

Emelio bucked his hips beneath her, driving heavily into her sodden heat. Her body clenched around him and his wrists strained against his bonds when he felt the first contractions in his shaft. Then, as a guttural moan was ripped from his throat, he exploded inside her.

His heart thundered in his chest and he lay beneath Stevie's glistening body, gasping for breath. After a few minutes, he became aware of the tingling numbness in his arms. "Hey, lady. Now that you've had your way with me, how about letting me go?"

"Thank you. That was so much better than my fantasy." She reached up and undid the knots. "How do you feel?"

"Incredible." Emelio wiggled his fingers, encouraging the blood to circulate to his fingers again. "I have to admit I was a little apprehensive at first. But then I let go, and when you made the decisions and set the pace, it was…really erotic."

Stevie leaned forward to press her lips to his, and he was mildly surprised by the tenderness of her kiss. "Thank you for trusting me, Emelio. As great as the sex was, I appreciated that even more."

He wasn't sure how he felt right now, but he knew that things had irrevocably altered between them. He recognized the change in her bright blue gaze and in his own turbulent emotions. She kissed him again and then drifted off. He lay awake, however, his thoughts too troubled for sleep.

He'd fallen for her. Against his better judgment, he'd fallen hard for her unbroken spirit and unique character, her fierce independence and quick sarcastic wit. He loved her and there was no sense in denying it. But what would he do about it?

NOT USUALLY A MORNING PERSON, Emelio got up with the dawn and kissed Stevie's slumbering form before pulling on an old pair of jeans, the pale denim softened by years of wear. Silently he walked barefoot through the house to the converted garage, brimming with the excitement of starting something new.

Dazzling radiance filtered through the frosted skylights as the sun rose overhead, warming the art studio as he stood in front of the easel. After an hour of preliminary sketching, he'd chosen to discard his sable brushes in favor of feeling the creativity flow through his hands.

He wiped viridian-green paint off of his hands with a clean rag before pouring a small pool of linseed oil onto the wooden artist's palette. Then he added a drop of yellow ochre to the cadmium yellow. After mixing them together, he smoothed the now transparent and glossy color onto the painting.

Brightly hued oils oozed between his fingers as he swirled the colors over the gesso-primed canvas. The stylized abstract was coming to life before his eyes and he knew he had Stevie to thank for his burst of inspiration. Being with her, he'd rediscovered joy and laughter, finally reconnecting with the person he hadn't been in a long time.

Though he'd visited Naples a few weeks earlier, he hadn't painted in months. Since Lina's death, he'd been withdrawn, not really living so much as existing within the boundaries of cold, empty remorse. Overtown had left him with persistent doubts about his instincts and his honor.

Knowing it was against the rules, he'd gotten involved in a physical liaison with his informant. Lina quickly fell in love with him, and he'd allowed himself to love her in return. He should have kept her safe, should never have let his emotions get in the way and put her at risk. If he'd been thinking with his head instead of his heart, he would have questioned the information she gave him.

He might have saved her....

But despite his resolve, he saw himself making the same mistake of letting emotion rule his decisions. What he felt for Stevie he had no business feeling. *Antes de Dios,* he had never wanted to find himself in this position again, had done everything he could to avoid it. And yet the past couple of days had changed him.

Stephanie had changed him.

He chose the tube of phthalo blue, noticing for the first time how closely it matched the color of his lover's eyes. He stood back from the canvas, assessing the finished work, damn pleased with what he saw. He'd created an abstract sunrise over the ocean, the horizon line following the curve of a woman's profile with bright strands radiating from her body.

"It's beautiful, Emelio. I think it may be the best work you've done." At the sound of her honeyed voice, he looked away from the painting to the woman who inspired it, the woman who'd brought pleasure and passion back into his life.

Stevie was curled up in the recliner, wearing only a cotton T-shirt and panties. Sunlight gleamed on her cap of tousled hair, glowed on her flawless skin as she regarded him. Meeting her eyes, he saw the admiration in her slate-blue gaze.

"Good morning. How long have you been there?"

"A while." She came to her feet and walked across the studio toward him. "I'm amazed, I really am.

What a gift to be able to create something so beautiful and evocative.''

Her words filled him with pride and, embarrassed, he felt heat steal onto his face. ''It's just a painting.''

''Yeah.'' She stroked her hand along his naked back. ''And Everest is just a mountain.''

''I'm flattered by the comparison.'' His chuckle turned into a hum of pleasure when she pressed her soft lips against his shoulder.

''Well, size does matter.'' Stevie reached down to cup the placket of his jeans. ''I'm so glad you're not the smock-and-beret type because, I have to tell you, all of those paint flecks are turning me on.''

He grinned at the absurdity of her statement and the hot desire in her gaze. The heavy throb of sexual need stirred in the pit of his stomach as she ran her hands over his bare chest, spreading droplets of primary color across his skin.

With his paint-smeared hands held carefully out to the side, he tilted his head down and teased her lips apart with his tongue. His mouth slanted over hers again and again until she opened for him. Then she claimed his mouth in a kiss that was raw and lusty and left him gasping for air.

''I want your hands on me, Emelio.''

''I've got paint—''

''I don't care.''

In the space of a heartbeat, Stevie found herself enveloped in his brawny arms. The heat of his body seared through the thin cotton of her shirt. Emelio made a rough, impatient sound in his throat as he held her to the distinct bulge of his erection. She pressed against him, rubbing her hardened nipples on his chest, until he slipped one denim-clad thigh between her legs.

The friction against her damp panties set off a firestorm of need that ignited in her belly and raced through her entire body. His large hand slid beneath her T-shirt to massage her breast, lightly pinching the nipple to a sensitive peak.

She laced her fingers behind his head, pulling him closer as she explored his mouth. His tongue traced sensual patterns around hers as heat spiraled in her womb. His wide, firm lips seared her with a kiss that was both giving and demanding. At an unspoken signal, they parted.

Stevie held his gaze, saw the golden sparks that leaped in his hazel eyes and shivered. She had to have him, right now. She yanked the T-shirt off then cocked her head toward the door.

"Bedroom?"

He shook his head as he peeled down his jeans. "Floor?"

She glanced over at the wall. "Sofa?"

"Table." When a surprised giggle escaped her, he grinned. "Black-lace letter number eight, remember?"

> Are you willing to indulge my fantasies, anytime, any place? You never know when I might grab your hand and just say, "now." If you would be spontaneous and wild, then I'd be yours in black lace....

"Yeah, I remember."

The look in his eyes literally made her quiver. Calm, cool and controlled? This man wore sexual magnetism as fire wore heat. In a lust-roughened voice he uttered a single word.

"Now."

Stevie managed to wiggle out of her panties mere seconds before Emelio lifted her into his arms. He carried her over to an old wooden table, worn smooth over the years. After settling her on the edge, he swept the sketch pads and charcoal pencils to the floor.

She lay back, eagerly anticipating his claiming. But instead he kneeled down in front of her. His strong hands gripped her knees while he nibbled a path to her inner thighs. The feel of his tongue licking hot circles on her bare flesh sent bolts of delight along her belly. She gasped as the sharp edges of his teeth grazed her tender skin.

Stevie moaned aloud at the first touch of his mouth. She instinctively wriggled her hips to meet his every touch. The rough sensation laving the tiny bud of nerves urged her toward a quickly escalating orgasm. When his tongue delved inside her and his mouth created a gentle suction, her vaginal muscles clenched and shuddered with pleasure.

When she reached for him, Emelio stood up and nestled the engorged head of his penis between her thighs. He gazed down at her, motionless, the seconds ticking by with each beat of her heart. Then he plunged into her, filling her to the hilt.

Stevie arched her back, crying out with each powerful thrust. She crossed her calves behind his back to hold him in place, but he surprised her by bringing her legs around and resting her ankles on his shoulders. With her legs braced along his body like this, it changed the whole angle of penetration, and she finally discovered the infamous G spot. Hoo yah.

Emelio flexed his hips, increasing the friction along with the pace. She grabbed the edge of the table with both hands to keep from banging her head on the wall. Molten fire flooded her. As the delicious contractions held him deep inside her, he surged forward, groaning his own release.

A moment later, she gingerly lowered her legs. Emelio pulled out and offered his hand to help her up. He led her across to the sofa, lay down and pulled her on top of him. He draped his arms around her back, gliding his fingers over her glistening skin, and closed his eyes.

Stevie sighed contentedly and turned to rest her cheek on his shoulder. Something between them had changed. The sex had been just as hot, just as extreme as before. But she sensed a poignant connection that had been missing from their earlier encounters. She relaxed under the soothing massage of his touch and let her gaze drift to the painting across the room.

The work was stunning, probably the best he'd done. The brilliant swirls of color were more personal—she could see where his hands had connected with the canvas—and the composition symbolized renewal, beginnings, rebirth.

Tears pricked her eyes even as a rush of warmth spread through her. Her therapist had advised her not to be afraid of her feelings, to acknowledge and even celebrate them. She could almost see the fireworks display. A brass marching band played for all it was worth. The notion of confetti and streamers filled her heart.

She wasn't ready for this. After warily controlling

her every emotion for so many years, she felt vulnerable, uncertain and unprepared for what was happening. But how could a woman with a shadowed past resist a man who created sunlight?

THEY'D FORGOTTEN the condoms.

Stevie hesitated to broach the subject. But, it had to be asked. She wrapped her hair in one of the thick towels in the master bath, glancing over when Emelio stepped out of the shower. Watching him dry the moisture from his magnificent body, she had to clear her throat before speaking.

"We should probably talk about, um, what just happened. We weren't too careful that time."

"I know." He winced. "Here I've been promising to keep you safe, but instead we got caught up in the moment."

Stevie reached for the bottle of lotion and braced herself. "Now that it's out in the open... I've only had sex with two people since leaving Tom, and I was excessively cautious with both of them. I need to know whether your, um, history, puts me at risk."

He grabbed a brush and swept his damp hair back from his forehead, avoiding her gaze in the mirror. "I was involved with someone two years ago, but I know Lina was healthy."

"How can you be so sure?"

Emelio hesitated and the room seemed stifling in the silence. "Lina was a virgin. She'd never been with anyone else."

Something painful pierced his expression just before shutters came down over his gaze. Stevie chose not to pursue it; she was uncertain whether she wanted to delve into that particular past.

'Okay, what about since then?"

He dropped the brush and moved toward the bedroom. "The other night, I told you a little about what happened after Overtown. I, uh, haven't dated much since then."

Stevie hung up the towel and followed him out of the bath. "That doesn't answer my question."

Emelio turned to cup her face between his palms. The look in his eyes was enigmatic, but tenderness infused his tone when he spoke. "There hasn't been anyone in my life since Lina. Not until you."

8

ROGELIO BRAGA STOOD at the picture window of his library. He looked out at the Atlantic but didn't notice the beauty of the day. His eyes were focused on the past. He saw Carolína's face the way he chose to remember her—untouched, unspoiled. The way she had looked before Sanchez corrupted her.

His sweet Carolína had been anxious to get away from Santo Domingo and experience the world. She'd come to America under his protection, with assurances to the family that he would educate her and see that she wanted for nothing.

Braga closed his eyes, remembering. He had showered her with attention and gifts, watching her blossom into a lovely young woman. And, in turn, Carolína had worshiped him, looking to him for guidance and affection. Over the years his desire for her had grown, but he'd held himself in check, reluctant to end her innocence too soon.

And then his plan had gone wrong, horribly wrong. Emelio Sanchez entered their lives, and Carolína discovered the truth about the travel agency, the money laundering and about Braga. Never would he forget the hatred and betrayal in her gaze. Nor could he obliterate the images of her writhing naked beneath Sanchez's rutting form.

He opened his eyes, cold fury churning inside him.

For the past two years he had beaten every charge brought against him. More importantly, he'd beaten Sanchez and bided his time. Now he was close, so very close to achieving his goals.

He had maneuvered in Frankie Ramos's shadow for too long, made too many sacrifices. All that he wanted was within his grasp. He would eliminate the head of the cartel and take Ramos's place, *his* rightful place.

He would also get his revenge. Emelio Sanchez thought he was smart. But Braga was smarter. He had no idea where they had run to, but he would find out. Sanchez and his woman believed themselves safe. It was an illusion he very much looked forward to destroying.

"LOOKING FOR MORE NECKTIES?"

While Emelio pulled on a clean pair of jeans and a cream-colored polo shirt, Stevie rummaged through his walk-in closet. He wouldn't refuse if she wanted to try light bondage herself this time.

"No, I'm putting on a disguise."

Hmm. Which black-lace letter was that from? "Don't bother, lady. I'd recognize you anywhere."

"Even dressed like this?"

He turned to look at her and couldn't help but grin. Despite her attempts to strut like a runway model, he didn't know of any designer who'd have sketched this particular outfit.

Stevie had on one of his rugby shirts, buttoned to the neck and hanging down to the middle of her thighs. At least he thought they were her thighs. She was wearing his baggiest sweatpants, too. A paisley bandana totally covered her hair and her eyes were hidden behind dark sunglasses. What made the outfit so comical was that his rugby shirt fit her.

"How did you manage to gain sixty pounds in the last ten minutes?"

"I'm wearing every T-shirt you own under here." Stevie flashed him a bright smile and patted her falsely ample hips.

"Should I even ask why you're dressed like that?"

A light flush colored her cheeks. "I may be stubborn, but I'm not stupid. I really want to tour Naples today and this is my way of being cautious."

Emelio crossed his arms. "Okay, you've done a hell of a job changing your profile and hiding your most notable features. But I'm still not sure—"

Her voice took on a steel edge. "Just know, I am leaving this house today. With or without you."

Like hell. Maybe she didn't take him seriously, but he wasn't about to put her at risk. He scowled at her. "Do you really think I'd let you go alone?"

"No, chér. I know you wouldn't." Stevie angled her head to one side, her expression apologetic and yet full of mischief. "That's why I've come up with a disguise for you, too."

A half hour later, Emelio caught his reflection in a store window and grimaced. Beneath an unbuttoned cotton shirt, his disguise consisted of only one T-shirt, but with the addition of a small pillow to conceal his lean build. He pulled the baseball cap a little lower over his eyes. "I don't remember James Bond ever wearing a getup like this."

"Sorry, but a tuxedo and handgun might have raised a few eyebrows."

The temperature was a cool sixty-five degrees in spite of the bright January sun reflecting off the pale sand-colored brick sidewalk. A light breeze carried the scents of sunshine and seawater, rustling the lush foliage. He decided the extra clothing wasn't so bad after all. But the pillow kept shifting, making his "beer belly" seem lumpy.

"Thanks for doing this." Stevie reached for his hand.

When she gave him that open, eager smile, he couldn't resist her and it was becoming more and more natural to smile back. Following an impulse, he ducked his head to brush a kiss over her cheek. As they strolled around historic Old Naples, Stevie's enthusiasm rubbed off on him, and he saw the area as though for the first time.

The quiet tree-lined streets with their contemporary Mediterranean architecture boasted a variety of upscale shops and restaurants. Yet there was still a quaint small-town atmosphere amid the landscaped oases and wrought-iron benches.

Emelio lead Stevie past the plaza on Third Street South. The murmuring of the double-heron fountain was broken by the occasional squawk of brightly hued parrots huddled in the towering banyan trees.

Without warning, Stevie squealed, tightening her grip on his hand. Adrenaline surged through his veins as he tried to identify the danger. His body tensed, preparing to defend her against any threat. Good thing he'd strapped the Ruger into his shoulder holster before leaving the cottage.

His voice was low and tight as he scanned the area. "What is it, Stephanie?"

"Your paintings!"

Emelio hissed through his clenched teeth and released the tension from his muscles. "Don't do that."

She winced and offered an apology. "Sorry. I forgot that it's a secret."

"No, I mean don't scare me like that again. I thought you saw something."

"I did! That gallery over there has one of your paintings on display."

He looked toward the shop she pointed out and saw that one of his early works was available from the Hillman-Grey Gallery. He hadn't known it was back on the market and so readily agreed when Stevie wanted to "check out how much you're worth."

"Wow, Emelio. This is great! I've read about this one in art books, but never thought I'd get to see it in person."

Seeing one of his first efforts again, he couldn't help but criticize. "The colors should have been bolder. And the brush strokes are too hesitant. Really, the whole composition could have been so much better."

A voice spoke from behind them. "You're obviously not familiar with Castillo's work."

Emelio turned to find a black-clad woman of a certain age eyeing them disdainfully. The discreet name tag on her lapel suggested Ms. Weatherly was an authority on modern art. Her remote glance took in their odd clothing, and he struggled not to cop an attitude of his own.

"I've seen Castillo's stuff before."

Ms. Weatherly looked down her patrician nose at them and smirked. "I'm *sure* you have."

He had to give Stevie credit for her self-control, even though her grip on his hand tightened again. "So how much are you asking for this one?"

"José Castillo is one of the premier artists of the

century. His early paintings are extremely rare and therefore very expensive.''

Stevie bared her teeth in what barely passed for a smile. ''How much?''

The manager named a figure that made her blanch, and even he was a little taken aback. After the gallery's commission and his agent's cut, he'd still see a generous increase in his bank-account balance.

Stevie looked at him with a wide grin, obviously having done some math of her own. ''You're buying lunch.''

THE HOSTESS at the Mangrove Grill Café on Fifth Avenue South greeted them with a friendly smile. She led them through the beige-and-black Art Deco dining room to a windowside table set for lunch. A waitress took their drink orders and brought out homemade plantain chips and mango salsa before leaving them alone.

''Nice place, Emelio. I'm surprised they let you in looking like that.'' She flicked the brim of his baseball cap.

''Me? What about you?'' He reached over to poke her well-padded shoulder. ''Business must be slow today. Normally, you'd never get seated during the peak tourism months.''

Stevie grinned and looked over the menu. ''So what exactly is Floribbean cuisine, anyway?''

''It's a fusion of Cuban, Caribbean and American foods, served Florida style.'' He choked on a swallow of his iced tea in response to her skeptical reaction. ''Trust me, it tastes great. Chef Amaral is really talented.''

She turned her head to look out the window, casually watching the passersby and thinking about the past few days. "Naples is beautiful and you live very well here. So why isn't this your permanent home?"

"Someday it will be—it's just a matter of when. Right now, I love what I do. Alex and I talked about forming our own agency for years and, with January Investigations doing so well, there's no reason to leave."

Stevie dipped another plantain into the salsa. "Did you always want to be in law enforcement?"

The corner of Emelio's mouth turned up in a self-depreciating smile. "Pretty much. My parents and I came from Cuba when I was six years old. Pápi always told us how lucky we were and how anything was possible here. He wanted me to be a doctor like him, and he hasn't really forgiven me for not continuing the family tradition. But even as a kid I wanted to protect the American dream."

She felt a little piece of her heart melt. How could you not love a guy who said that with a straight face? She leaned her elbows on the table, interested in hearing more. "Was your father upset that you didn't follow in his footsteps?"

"When I first told him I was going to major in criminology instead of premed, he was very disappointed." Emelio waited until their waitress had written down their choices of entrée before continuing. "By the time I got to the FBI Academy at Quantico, though, my sister Connie was on her way to a career in pediatrics. She works at North County General."

Stevie raised her eyebrows. "Rough neighborhood. What about your other sisters? What do they do?"

"Angie is a social worker in the child-welfare department. I worry about some of the areas she has to visit, but she's very dedicated to her job. And then there's Maggie. She's a reporter for WPLG local news now, with dreams of becoming a foreign correspondent. If that happens, I'll never get any sleep."

Stevie watched several expressions cross his features and couldn't believe she'd ever thought him distant. Having gotten to know him outside of the office, she could easily recognize his pride and love and concern. She felt a sharp prickle of envy—her brother Eric had never given a damn about her.

"Why don't you want Maggie to follow her dream?"

Emelio wiped a smear of salsa from his lip. "I'd worry too much. I have enough problems keeping track of my sisters, even though they all still live at home."

"They do?"

"It's expected that nice Cuban girls stay with their parents until marriage. As I said before, my mother has old-fashioned values. Just the same, Connie works at a knife-and-gun club, right in the middle of gang territory. Angie is always chasing cop cars and ambulances. If Maggie got assigned to some war-torn desert…"

Their waitress appeared with the entrées, setting a plate of portobello mushrooms stuffed with Havarti cheese and chorizo by Emelio and put the steak salad over black beans and couscous in front of Stevie. As she picked up her fork, a family being shown past their table caught her attention.

The young woman pushed an infant in a stroller, a dark-haired baby lay peacefully on a yellow blanket, her big bright eyes taking in the world around her.

Gazing at the beautiful child caused Stevie an unexpected pang of yearning and envy.

"I just want you to know that I'll be there, if you need me. That I'll do the right thing."

She turned her attention from the baby to Emelio. "What are you talking about?"

His gaze was steady within a serious expression. "Is there any chance you could get pregnant?"

"No." Her reply was immediate and emphatic.

"How can you be so sure?"

She refused to meet his eye or to dwell on the awful memories. "My ex never managed it, despite numerous attempts."

As always, Emelio heard what she didn't say. "I'm sorry."

In the years she was married to Tom, she'd never once conceived. As it turned out, she could only be grateful they'd had no children or she might never have been able to leave him. Now, though, she wondered for the first time if the failing had been Tom's, and not hers after all.

When Emelio grasped her fingers, she looked up into the earnestness of his gaze and she suddenly felt trapped. His melodic voice held notes of quiet reassurance. "I come from a large, close-knit family and someday I want a family of my own. If you were to get pregnant, I would of course marry you and give our child my name."

Pregnant. Was it possible? Her pulse roared in her ears and she'd suddenly lost her appetite, but she tried to hide her distress. She racked her brain, trying to remember whether ovulation took place the second week after menstruation or the third? And which week was she on anyway?

It took all of her effort not to give in to the urgent desire to scream or throw something or just cry. Instead, she eased her hand away and leaned back in her chair. "You could try asking, you know."

Emelio's eyebrows furrowed at the edge in her voice. "It's a little early for a proposal—"

"Don't make assumptions. And don't make any more decisions for me."

"Relax, Stephanie." He picked up his fork, giving her some space both emotionally and physically. "Let's not worry before we have to. I just thought we should talk about it."

Stevie pushed the remaining food around her plate, no longer hungry. She concentrated on identifying the emotions running amok. *Sheepish.* Two otherwise responsible adults should have known better than to forget a condom in this day and age. And, oh, in her most secret heart of hearts was a glimmering spark of *hope.*

But mostly she felt *scared.* She'd already been her parents' daughter, then Tom's trophy. If she were to get pregnant, she'd instantly become Emelio's wife and the baby's mother. When would she ever be Stevie again?

She'd fallen in love with him. There. She admitted it. But in loving him, would she disappear? In that moment of clarity, Emelio had become almost as much of a threat to her as Braga. Either way she could lose her life.

OUTSIDE OF THE RESTAURANT, Emelio captured Stevie's hand and tugged her closer to him. Her usual bright, restless energy had dimmed considerably during their lunch. He could only assume she was thinking about the possibility of pregnancy. Emelio wasn't sure how he felt about that himself. It would be one hell of a change to his job and his lifestyle.

He reached up to smooth the lines between her eyebrows before sweeping a kiss over her pouting lips. "So, Stephanie. What would you like to do next?"

She gave a little shrug. Not an easy gesture underneath all of those layers of her disguise. "I don't know. Why don't you give me a few ideas."

"We could walk down to the pier and look for dolphins. Or I could find a cab and we could go shopping at the Village on Venetian Bay. Or—" His cell phone rang, the musical chimes muffled inside several shirts. "Or I could answer the phone."

He dug it out of his pocket while Stevie gazed at the passersby and pretended not to eavesdrop. Alex barely waited for his greeting. "Where are you, Em?"

"Hey. We're just walking around disguised as tourists."

"Well, duck and cover, partner. You've got trouble."

Stevie gave a startled gasp as he grabbed her hand and rushed back inside the Mangrove Café. Her eyebrows drew together in a questioning look as they hid inside the entryway, but he merely shook his head. He'd explain once he understood what was going on.

"What's happened, Alex?"

"I saw the news. A couple of women were assaulted in Fort Myers. They were all tall, athletic blondes with short hair."

Emelio didn't believe in coincidence. He dropped his chin, briefly closing his eyes as he recognized the full extent of the danger. "*Mierda.* That's only forty-five miles north of here."

"Ditch this phone. Braga must have gotten a trace on it somehow, at least to the nearest cellular routing station."

He angled his head to catch Stevie's eye. "You've got a mobile phone, don't you?"

"Yeah," she nodded. "In my suitcase."

Emelio spoke to Alex. "I've got another one at the cottage. I'll call you back with the number."

He clicked off the connection and sighed heavily. Though he stood motionless, his mind raced to ascertain their options and decide on a plan of action.

"What's going on? What did Alex say?" Stevie kept her voice low and urgent as the restaurant hostess stole a curious glance in their direction.

"It looks like Braga may have tracked us as far as Fort Myers. We've got to get off the street."

Color drained from her face, making her slate-blue eyes appear huge against the pallor of her skin. Emelio cupped her cheek in one palm, infusing his tone with as much reassurance as he could. "I'll never let him get to you."

She readily came into his embrace. "What do we do now?"

"Get back to the house. We should be safe there for the rest of today. From Fort Myers they'll have to search Marco Island, Sanibel and Cape Coral before they get to Naples. But just the same, we need to find another place to stay."

BACK AT THE COTTAGE, Emelio watched Stevie stalk across the living room while he dialed Alex on her mobile phone. She paced like a caged tigress, waiting for the opportunity to snarl and take a chomp out of something.

"Think, Stevie. You said you never forget a face. When did you see Braga before? Where were you? What were you doing? You've got to try and remember."

She shoved an ottoman out of the way with her foot. "Leave me alone. I can't think and answer you at the same time."

He left her alone. But at some point he was going to suggest anger management. That woman had a hell of a temper when she felt out of control.

Meanwhile, he walked across the hallway to his office. Emelio booted up his computer and did an Internet search of news articles. He jotted notes on a legal pad, trying to determine where Braga had been over the past months. Later he'd check with Stevie to see where their paths might have crossed.

An hour passed before he knew it. He logged off the computer and sat back, rubbing his eyes. Braga was slick and he covered his tracks well. Without having access to the databases at the FBI anymore, the only information he could find was pretentious accounts of Braga's legitimate business dealings and charitable contributions.

Emelio knew better, though. He knew what Braga was capable of. A callous manipulator and a consummate liar, he'd involved members of his own family in the cartel's business. He'd orchestrated a takeover and let Ramos take the fall at Cayo Sueño. Nothing and no one stood in the way of his ambition.

Braga apparently didn't see it that way, though. For some reason, he considered Stevie a serious enough threat to send people hunting across the state. She'd spent hours at his laptop reading through her case files, but nothing in them had explained why Braga was stalking her.

They had to be out of the cottage by tomorrow morning. He needed to make arrangements for a safe place to take her. He was just about to make some calls when Stevie wandered into the office. "Should you be using that phone anymore?"

Emelio put down the receiver and reached for her. "It's set up as a business line listed as Castle Consulting Services. It can't be traced to me personally."

As she settled on his lap, he saw that her complexion had returned to its normal vivid appearance. The lines of tension had eased from her forehead, but shadows still haunted her eyes, leaving them more gray than blue.

"Feeling better now?"

"No, but I'll get through it." Stevie sighed heavily and leaned her forehead against his. "I guess our little vacation from reality is over, huh?"

"What do you mean?"

"For the past few days, I was able to pretend we were just two people getting to know each other. Now, the danger is back. We have to run. We have to hide." Her shoulder muscles tensed and her voice sounded strained. "I just want this to be over. I just want to get back to my life."

"We'll figure it out, don't worry." Emelio stroked his palm over her hair and kissed her temple. "And I promise you this, Braga isn't going to get anywhere near you."

9

EMELIO'S HAND WAS REACHING under the pillow for his gun even before he'd come fully awake. The persistent buzzing noise had roused him from a fitful sleep. His heart thundered in his chest as he rolled off the bed into darkness, crouching below the level of the windows.

He had to move. In about thirty seconds, that buzzing would change to a high-pitched shriek of sound when the security alarm fully engaged. He had to get Stevie out of the house before whoever was breaking in found her.

At the end of the bed, his pulse shuddered as he bumped into another body. The smell of her sleep-warmed skin was the only thing that kept Stevie from getting knocked on her ass. She was crouched down, as well, and he could barely hear her whisper when she spoke.

"We've got visitors, Emelio."

"Stay down. They may have nightscopes."

He felt her tense beside him, but she remained low to the floor. "What's the plan?"

"I'm going to do a quick recon, determine which way they're coming in. Then I'll get you out of here."

"I'll get myself out. You don't know how many there are."

"Stephanie—"

The buzzing ceased abruptly. The wires had been cut. It was the only way to deactivate the system from outside.

Emelio's heart pounded as adrenaline poured into his system. Should he uphold his honor or follow his instincts? He was torn between wanting to head off Braga's minions and needing to keep Stevie safe.

Honor be damned, just once. This was his chance to get back in the game. "Stay here."

Her hiss of protest was immediate. "No way!"

The backup alarm would go off any second now, flooding the grounds with light and alerting the intruders they'd been caught. He grabbed her arm, whispering harshly. "I mean it, Stevie. I don't want to shoot you in the dark."

"Damn it, Emelio. I can do my job! I've been trained—"

He gave her a gentle push, knocking her on her ass after all. "You can tell me about your Hostile Infiltration classes later. Right now, I have to know you'll be safe. *Stay here.*"

Gripping the .45 caliber tightly, he jogged barefoot out of the bedroom and along the gloomy hallway. Listening carefully, he cursed the light color of his sleep pants—the pale fabric would easily be seen in the darkness.

There. Emelio jerked his head in the direction of a slight scraping noise. They had gotten through the pool enclosure and were now trying to gain entrance to the house itself. He flicked the safety off the Ruger and headed for the back door, praying his footsteps weren't as loud as they sounded in his mind.

The intruders probably thought the alarm system was already disabled, not realizing that as soon as the wire was tripped a call went out to the local authorities. He just hoped he got to them before the cops came. He was spoiling for a fight and he needed whatever information he could either overhear or beat out of someone.

Suddenly, the backup alarm screamed to life and floodlights turned the night into high noon. He took advantage of the intruder's surprise-induced paralysis and flung the door open. In the moment they stood face-to-face, Emelio determined that the guy was alone at this entrance, he wasn't one of Braga's regular henchmen, and that he was under the influence.

The intruder spun around and dashed across the lanai. Moment over. Emelio was hard on his heels when the guy caught his leg against one of the lounge chairs. It was all Emelio needed to get hold of a fistful of black turtleneck and yank the guy off his feet.

"Where are the others?"

"There's nobody—"

He rapped the intruder's jaw with the barrel of the gun to ensure his undivided attention. Judging by how dilated the guy's pupils were, Emelio had to be certain he was getting through.

"Answer me! Where are they?"

"I came alone, I swear! There's no one else."

Screeech. A terra-cotta planter scraped against the patio tile. His breath caught as he automatically turned toward the sound. He was an open target, standing here under the lights in his pajamas. Scanning the perimeter, Emelio damned his inability to see past the floodlights.

Shards of glass rained onto the lanai when he shot out the halogen bulbs above the pool. A second later, the darkness exploded into a thousand stars of pain when the intruder's knee connected with his groin. Emelio fought the nausea as he cupped himself and staggered back a step. His attacker gave him a hard shove then took off again, flying through the propped-open door to the pool enclosure.

Every fiber of Emelio's being urged him to follow the guy onto the beach. But both his injury and his concern for Stevie made him hesitate. He shouldn't have left her unprotected. As he turned to go back inside the cottage, however, a pale blur of motion caught his eye.

Madre de Dios. None of Braga's men had short blond hair or long, shapely legs or wore his pajama shirt to bed. He hobbled after Stevie, cursing savagely. He was going to kill her if those guys didn't do it first. She was running flat out along the dunes…toward the intruder.

Despite the fear stabbing his gut, he also felt a surge of pride because damned if she wasn't gaining on the guy. With a leap right out of an action movie, she made a flying tackle and finally brought him down. The two of them were wrestling on the ground when the intruder suddenly delivered a blow to Stevie's solar plexus. As she sank to her knees, the guy got up and sprinted toward the surf.

Rage added fuel to his stride as Emelio raced over the sand. She was hurt. That bastard had punched her and, in doing so, made the worst mistake of his life. He lost precious seconds while he checked on Stevie, who was gasping like a fish out of water. Knowing from experience that she'd be fine in a minute, he tore ass after her assailant.

The wail of sirens carried on the night air. Time was running out. It was a one-in-a-hundred shot, given the fifteen yards between them, but Emelio took it. The report was still echoing when the intruder stumbled, grabbing his leg where the slug ripped through his left thigh.

Emelio closed the distance and stood over the guy, the Ruger trained for a second shot if necessary. He swiftly checked the surroundings again. Either this guy really is alone or the others had gotten in the wind. Fixing his gaze on the wounded man, he called over to Stevie.

"You have to get up." A quick glance told him she hadn't moved. Or that she couldn't. "Get up, Jayne! I know it hurts, but you've got to go and stall the cops."

Out of the corner of his eye, he saw her finally raise her head and look in his direction. She struggled to her feet, bracing her palms on her hips and still gasping for air. She only managed a single word.

"Why?"

"I need answers and the Collier County sheriff isn't going to like how I get them."

IT LOOKED SO MUCH EASIER in the James Bond movies.

Standing at the living-room window, watching the ambulance and police cruisers pull out of the driveway, Stevie gingerly rubbed the aching bruise on her abdomen.

After emerging through the French doors from the bedroom, she'd dashed around the hot tub and across the patio. The terra-cotta planter was heavier than it looked, but she'd finally moved it and vaulted the brick wall.

She'd been so proud of herself when she caught

the bad guy on the beach behind the house. Then he'd knocked the breath out of her and all of her training fled. The blow had brought memories as well as pain.

Doubled over on the sand, she'd felt completely vulnerable. Again. And that had sent her temper soaring. After insisting to Emelio that she could handle herself, the first chance to put theory into practice had been a dismal failure.

At least the other guy looked worse. Their midnight visitor was sporting a blackened eye, a busted lip and a bullet in the leg. Despite all of that, the intruder kept denying any connection to Braga.

After finding night-vision goggles and burglar's tools in the prowler's backpack, the sheriff's deputies had also located a dinghy hidden in the tall grass near the shore. Since there had been a rash of break-ins around Naples over the past few months, the sheriff chose to believe the most obvious explanation. Case closed.

Emelio wasn't buying it, though. She felt the anger and frustration radiating off him in hot waves. "Get packed, Stevie. We're out of here."

"Where are we—?"

"*Virgen de la Caridad!*" His eyebrows slammed together in a scowl. "Could you just once follow instructions?"

She'd never seen him like this—he'd never directed real anger toward her before. Stevie hated to admit that her first instinct was a rush of fear and the urge to recoil. It lasted less than a second, but that gut reaction, after working so hard to outrun her past, was enough to set her temper off again.

"Kiss my ass, Emelio. If I had followed instructions, we never would have caught that guy."

Oh, had she hit a raw target. The color drained from his face even as fire lit his amber-green eyes, but he visibly struggled to rein in his own temper. That show of self-control completely dissolved any lingering fear and gave her the green light to get right in his face.

"Never split up the team when you have no idea what you're up against. That's the first thing we learned in my Urban First Response class. Lucky for us he was just a burglar!"

"You and your goddamn classes. You can take paramilitary international super-spy courses from now until you die, but they'll never replace common sense or instincts honed from years of experience."

"How am I supposed to gain any experience with you constantly trying to shut me in a cushioned box?"

"You could start by taking advice, orders and directions."

She knew she'd screwed up tonight and that she was damn lucky that guy didn't work for Braga. The bruises would be painful reminders over the next few days. But she still resented the fact that he didn't consider her a real partner.

"You know what your problem is? You always have to be the hero. You're not happy unless the weight of the world is on your oh-so-responsible shoulders. It just kills you not to be in control!"

"Look who's talking!" The closed-off expression on Emelio's face told her he was still struggling with his temper. "No, Stephanie, what killed me was seeing you get hurt. How do you think I felt watching that guy punch you, knowing it could have been avoided if you had stayed in the bedroom..."

His gaze dropped to where her hand still soothed the bruises. Then the anger drained from his expression and he closed his eyes briefly. "It wouldn't have happened if I'd done my job."

Her own defensiveness faded, as well, and she reached out to touch his arm. "What is this really about?"

"I should have protected you." Emelio brushed his fingers along her cheek. "With the exception of some phone calls and a little Internet searching, I haven't been able to do much on this case. So tonight, when given the chance to find out the extent of Braga's threat, I made the wrong choice."

She dropped her chin, tilting her face to the palm of his hand. "You're not the only one who made a wrong choice. As usual, I followed my impulses. I wanted so badly to prove myself, to show you I could do the job, that I put myself in danger. It's my own fault that I got hurt."

Emelio opened his arms and she moved gratefully into his embrace. She laid her cheek against his bare chest, felt the heat of his body melt away the tension.

"How are you feeling?"

"Oh, I've been worse. But I think I'm going to have to turn in my secret-agent decoder ring." It had been an emotionally draining day and all she really wanted was to go back to sleep. But they had several hours of driving ahead.

"So, where are we going, chér?"

"Back to Miami. We're going to hide in plain sight."

THEY'D TAKEN THE INTERSTATE highway this time, but Emelio still wouldn't let her drive. So Stevie had slept for the past two hours, waking up as they exited I-95 South and turned onto Seventh Street.

"Where are we?"

"Little Havana. I keep a place here."

She shook her head and brushed at the wrinkles in the leaf-green skirt she'd grabbed off the bedroom floor before they left. "Let me get this straight. You keep a 'cottage' in Naples. And now I find out that you also keep 'a place' in Little Havana. Even though you already have a home in Coral Gables."

"Don't worry, the lease isn't under my name. It's like a safe house. We use the apartment to meet with informants or to baby-sit witnesses before they testify."

She rubbed an ache in her neck, the result of sleeping with her head against the Jeep's passenger window. "You know, most people keep pets, not real estate."

"Real estate doesn't chew up the furniture."

As they drove along, Stevie caught glimpses of crowded sidewalks and still-lit storefronts from between concrete buildings painted in colors like turquoise, lime and white. "Is it always this lively at two o'clock in the morning?"

"Last night was *viernes culturales*. On the last Friday of every month, *Calle Ocho,* Southwest Eighth Street, hosts a street festival with dancing, art displays and sidewalk vendors."

Music seemed to surround her. Heavy bass beats erupted from passing cars while fiery merengue melodies beckoned from nightclubs. Street signs announced their location in English and *en Español.* The air smelled of unfamiliar spices and excitement. It wasn't so much like driving into another part of Miami as entering a different world.

A few minutes and several turns later, Emelio parked in front of a coral-orange building. On the corner was a small grocer, what he called *una bodega.* He promised to get café Cubano and guava pastries when the store opened in a few hours. Stevie followed him up the narrow stairs to a clean but musty third-floor apartment.

She looked around at the cramped living room, tiny kitchen and short hallway leading to a single bedroom. The layout wasn't much different from her own apartment, but the bare walls and sparse furnishings made it clear no one really lived here.

"Make yourself at home, such as it is."

"Oh, I don't know, chér. With a few plants, a good dusting and some cheap travel posters, this place would perk right up."

Emelio put her suitcase and the duffel bag he'd packed near the lumpy-looking sofa and set his laptop computer on the small desk. While he unstrapped his shoulder holster, she went over to open the terrace door and let in some fresh air.

Stevie stood on the narrow wrought-iron balcony, looking down on the darkened street and listening to the rhythmic percussion of numerous drums and the fainter strumming of guitars. She cocked her head when she sensed Emelio behind her.

"What is that music?"

"That's a *rumba,* a Cuban jam-session party. Delgado's is just over on Sixth." He draped one arm around her waist, pulling her back against his chest. "The band is just warming up. Some nights they play until dawn."

"Now that sounds like a great idea." Stevie turned to wrap her arms behind his neck, gently rubbing her pelvis across his.

A slight smile of amused interest pulled at the corners of his mouth. "Dawn isn't for another five hours."

"That's plenty of time for black-lace letter number seven."

In my fantasy, my body is covered with nothing but the elements and you. A sultry summer night's breeze is all that comes between us as we make love on the lawn. My heartbeat quickens with the thrill of getting caught....

"Sorry, Stephanie. It's a little chilly out here and there's no grass—"

"Spoilsport."

Emelio moved forward, trapping her between the hard metal rail and the hard heat inside his jeans. He bent his head to nibble the side of her neck, his voice a low growl in her ear. "If you're sure that's what you want, I'll take you right here on the balcony, right now."

A gasp of surprise and excitement escaped her. It was just a fantasy—she never thought he'd actually be willing. But if Emelio wanted to try it... She moaned as he cupped her breast.

"Turn around, Stephanie. I'll lean you over the railing, lift your skirt and pull your panties to one side. Then I'll push myself inside you, taking you hard and fast and deep, until you scream your orgasm into the night."

Stevie felt dampness flood the apex of her thighs

as her pulse thundered along her veins. Her body was on fire from wanting him, vibrating with lust. She clasped the sides of his face and gave him a kiss that branded his taste onto her lips.

When she finally came up for air, he looked at her with desire and something more in his expression. Fatigue. She couldn't ignore how tired she was, either, and so she offered him a conciliatory smile. "Number seven can wait for another time. Maybe you'd rather go inside and be comfortable on the bed."

"Hmm. There's a lot to be said for the comfortable approach. I can undress you completely, then take my time kissing every single inch of your beautiful body. I'll make love to you slowly, thoroughly, until you come apart in my arms."

Emelio took Stevie's hand and led her through the apartment, stopping only to grab a condom from his duffel bag. In the small bedroom, they stripped quickly and kissed slowly. He brushed his lips over hers, savoring their velvet warmth. She pressed closer, opening to the gentle invasion of his tongue.

Unlike their last encounter, when fulfilling her fantasy in black-lace letter number six had damn near drowned them both in the cottage pool, Emelio took his time seducing her. The heat between them built gradually, a warm glow as opposed to a raging fire, the heat of tenderness as well as desire.

He eased her onto the bed then joined her on the thin cotton quilt. Stevie reached for him in the muted light filtering through the heavy curtains. She whispered encouragement as his body covered hers and she arched her hips to meet him. He entered her in one smooth motion, merging their bodies in the darkness.

Emelio supported his weight on his elbows, watching her face as he flexed inside her. Even in the dim light, he could see the emotion in her gaze. Stevie's hands caressed his naked back, her touch telling him all he needed to know. Together they found their unique rhythm, urging each other to greater depths of desire.

Beneath him, Emelio felt Stevie surrender to the growing passion. It was only now, only when making love, that she would let go and give him any control. He repositioned his body, taking his entire weight on his arms and moving higher on the bed to change the angle of penetration. Stevie raised her head and traced her tongue around his left nipple.

He rocked forward so that his shaft rubbed against her clitoris, plunging deeper and faster until she cried out with the power of her orgasm. Tremors rocked his body when he finally allowed himself to follow her over the edge. The pleasure of his release was pure and explosive.

After a few minutes, his breathing slowed and he shifted onto his side. Stevie lay trembling in his embrace, her heart pounding against his chest. Emelio cuddled her closer until she drifted off. He doubted he'd be able to sleep at all. He felt drained, weary in a way that wasn't physical.

Braga was upping the ante.

How the hell did he manage to hunt them to Naples? Emelio's thoughts twisted in confused circles. Where had he failed Stevie? At what point had he let down his guard?

Beside him, she murmured softly in her sleep and

he sighed. It honest to God scared him how much he loved her. He knew in his heart he'd go to any extreme to keep her safe. Even if that meant backing off for a while in order to make the right decisions. He had to put aside his feelings and try to remain professional. He couldn't put her at risk again.

LATER THAT MORNING, after a long, hot shower, Stevie dressed in a fresh lavender T-shirt and paisley skirt before padding barefoot out to the living room. Emelio was sitting at the desk, his fingers flying over the laptop's keyboard. He wore the same aqua polo shirt and jeans he'd had on last night.

Stevie moved up behind him, draping her arms over his shoulders. "Good morning. Why did you let me sleep so late?"

"Guess I lost track of time."

At the raspy sound of his voice, she leaned down to get a good look at his face. His eyes were bloodshot and the coffee-brown waves of his hair lay in furrows from where his fingers had raked through the strands. His skin was pale, making the rough stubble on his jaw stand out in stark relief.

"You haven't been to sleep yet."

"Soon. I'm still trying to find out some leads." He reached up to rub his eyes. Then he took her left hand and absently kissed her fingers.

She kneaded his shoulders, trying to ease the knots of tension. "I don't suppose anything I could say would convince you to stop and get some rest?"

He glanced up at her with a tired smile. "I took a break an hour ago and got coffee and pastries. They're in the kitchen."

She started to insist he go to sleep, only to have

her belly interrupt. ''Thanks, Emelio. And I don't just mean for breakfast.''

As she turned toward the kitchenette, his attention was already back on the lines of text scrolling down the computer screen. Stevie poured the foam cup of strong-smelling Cuban coffee into a mug she found in the cabinet, then popped it into the microwave along with the pastries.

Walking back out four minutes later, she swallowed the last bite of her first pastry. Emelio was still engrossed in his search. With no phone and only one computer, there wasn't much she could do to help.

''Mind if I switch on the TV?''

''No, go ahead.'' He tossed the answer over his shoulder. ''The Turner Network is still showing the James Bond movie marathon.''

''Great! I hope I didn't miss *From Russia With Love.* That's the one with the cigarette-boat chase scene.''

''Is that why you took the Maritime Endurance class?''

''Hey, you never know when you might need to use a flare gun to set off exploding oil drums and triumph over the evil forces from SPECTRE.''

Stevie flipped on the television then settled on the sofa with her coffee mug in one hand and the remote control in the other. She was shifting around, trying to find the softest lump, when the voice from the screen caught her attention.

''Alleged drug kingpin, Francisco Guillermo Ramos, is dead. This, and other news, when we return.''

10

"WHAT?!"

Emelio sounded as if he was strangling. As a commercial for new and improved deodorant protection flashed onto the screen, he reached over the back of the sofa and grabbed the remote control from her. He sped through the channels until he found another station broadcasting a late-morning news program.

"The top story at this hour is the apparent suicide of Francisco Guillermo Ramos. The purported head of the Dominican cartel was arrested last year at a Florida Keys resort on several counts of drug trafficking and money laundering. After numerous delays, his trial began almost a month ago. Ramos, scheduled to testify next week, was discovered earlier this morning hanging from the balcony of his hotel room."

"Three years wasted. Three years!" Emelio hurled the remote, shattering it against the wall. "Ramos made a deal with the Justice Department, then didn't have the guts to take the stand. *Maldiga ese bastardo al infierno.* All of our time and effort comes to nothing!"

Stevie reached out a comforting hand, knowing there was nothing she could say, but he shook her off. She gazed at him for a moment, saw the anger, disbelief and frustration, and decided to give him some space.

Turning back to the TV, she glanced down at the caption to see that Jack Weston, Assistant State's Attorney, was being interviewed. Then she looked up at his face. An itchy, tingling sense of recognition crawled along her nerves. Weston had the look of a typical all-American politician—blond hair, blond features, bland eyes—but part of her mind was screaming at her to look harder...

"Mr. Weston, can you tell us what the State's Attorney plans to do now?"

"Obviously, with Francisco Ramos dead, there's no point in continuing the trial. However, this unfortunate incident does nothing to sway the resolve of this office. The Ramos trial may be over, but the war on drugs will continue. We cannot allow—"

"I remember."

"Hmm?" Emelio stood beside the sofa, arms crossed tightly over his chest.

"I remember! I saw him, I saw Weston with Braga!"

He stared at her, then at the television and back again, frown lines marring his forehead. "That guy?"

"I'm sure of it."

"No, he couldn't—"

Stevie held up one palm to interrupt. "I told you, I never forget a face. But I couldn't place Braga's until I saw Weston."

She had Emelio's full attention now, his focus intent as he stared at her. "Tell me what you remember."

Stevie spoke carefully so that the images reeling through her mind came out as coherent sentences. "It was before Christmas. The Stocktons were having a big party and wanted to make sure the new security system we installed was working.''

''Why wouldn't it be?''

''The clients had us put in some sophisticated upgrades like motion sensors on the artwork and infrared in the room where they keep the safe.'' She made a sweeping gesture. That wasn't the important part. ''Anyway, when an alarm was tripped in one of the upstairs bedrooms, it was my turn to discourage amorous couples looking for a place to have illicit sex.''

Emelio snorted, familiar with the situation. ''Go on.''

''When I opened the door, I walked in on two men deep in conversation. They shook hands, like they'd just closed a deal. I *saw* Braga shake hands with Weston, the guy who's helping to prosecute his boss, Frankie Ramos.''

Emelio closed his eyes and swore again viciously.

Stevie leaned forward, elated that she had finally made the association. ''Weston must be part of the cartel. He's probably been helping Braga from the inside.''

''Christ, I can't believe this!'' He raised both arms and squeezed his temples between his palms. ''I have no idea how many cases against the cartel were lost on legal technicalities. I don't know what evidence might have been misplaced or destroyed, which witnesses Braga may have gotten to.... Shit!''

Stevie's heart beat erratically in her chest as she realized the full import of what she'd seen. ''If I saw them long enough to recognize *their* faces—''

''Then you were in the room long enough for them to memorize yours.'' His expression was grim. ''They saw you, Stephanie, and they've been stalking you ever since. That's why Braga sent the photos—to let you know he'd found out where you live."

Tendrils of fear curled like black ribbons through her veins. She hated being afraid. But she wasn't about to back down. "I won't let that keep me from signing an affidavit. I'll swear in court to what I saw."

Admiration shone in Emelio's eyes, but she also saw his hesitation. "Your seeing them together is damning enough to start an investigation, but not enough to hang them on. Did you hear anything they said?"

"I didn't hear much. They stopped talking as soon as I opened the door, but I know how to find out."

"There's another witness?" His features lit up with hope.

Stevie allowed a slow, triumphant grin to spread across her face. "Yeah, one with an unblinking eye. When I redesigned the security system, the client had audio and video surveillance installed in almost every room of the house. I didn't ask why, but I'm sure that party was recorded. All we have to do is get the videotapes."

Her pulse quickened for a different reason now. She knew Emelio was upset, but she couldn't contain her own growing excitement. She'd solved her own case, and she was finally going to get the chance to do real investigation work.

However, he didn't return her smile. "Wait a minute. We don't know for certain that there is a tape. And even if there was, we don't know for how long they're archived. The client might just use the same one over again."

Stevie refused to consider the possibility and let it

dampen her mood. Her first covert mission would involve going after a crime lord. Cool. ''It'll be easy enough to find out. Hand me my purse, will you? The Stockton's address should be in my handheld organizer.''

As he passed the bag over from the desk, a metallic voice from his laptop computer announced he had urgent mail. Startled, Stevie let the purse slip from her grasp. She crouched down to gather her wallet, checkbook and makeup bag.

From behind her, Emelio spoke quietly. ''I've got to get you out of Miami, preferably out of the state.''

''What? I'm not going anywhere.'' Stevie stood up and whipped around to look at him. His back was to her, blocking the laptop. ''It's over now. It has to be. Braga can't threaten us once we confront him with the surveillance video.''

When Emelio turned, she was stunned to see the anguished expression on his face. The pallor of his skin, already pale, now looked ashen as the last of his confidence drained away.

''It's not over.''

He moved aside and gestured toward the computer. Her gaze followed the line of his arm and her heart stopped. Stevie dropped her purse on the sofa and moved around in order to see the laptop clearly. Her throat constricted and she forgot to breathe. Stevie stared at the images glowing from the screen.

It was black-lace letter number six.

She and Emelio were making love in the swimming pool behind the cottage. Whoever had them under surveillance had used a telescopic lens, zooming in close enough to see the hard peaks of her nipples, the droplets of water on Emelio's skin. God only knew how long they'd been watched—the pictures showed them in several different positions and states of ecstasy.

"Apparently another manila envelope was delivered to the office. Alex scanned the pictures and sent them as attachments."

Stevie swallowed hard, appalled that the fulfillment of her sensual fantasy had been turned into some kind of pornographic threat. "How? How in the hell did he find us?"

"It's possible that intruder really was a burglar, but the timing is suspect. Maybe he was a decoy or a warning... I don't know. I can't think." Emelio groaned, and threw his head back. "Weston called my cell phone that first night in Naples."

"What? What did he want?"

He shook his head. "He was trying to figure out where I was, supposedly for rebuttal testimony. Obviously Weston wanted to locate us for Braga."

Stevie crossed her arms over her waist, almost numb from the onslaught of information. "That would explain the attacks in Fort Myers. But how did he find us at the cottage?"

Emelio reached over and manipulated the keyboard until the screen returned to the e-mail program. "There's another picture. This is the one that made the connection. I guess my agent sent out press kits to drive up the price of that early painting."

The digitalized image of a torn paper appeared. When the view enlarged, Emelio's likeness filled the screen. Below it was a caption about the Hillman-Grey Gallery's special presentation of the early works of José Castillo. Stevie didn't bother reading the rest of the article.

"I hate this!" She swung away from the sofa, needing to move. Her eyes watered and panic threatened to break her down. It was happening again. A man's will was closing in on her, trapping her in a state of desperation and fear.

No. Not again. She stalked back across the room. Calling upon hard-learned survival skills, she quickly tapped into her anger. While fear might paralyze her, fury would give her the strength to get through this. "We have to get that videotape. If I don't take a stand now, Braga wins."

Emelio shook his head, sighing heavily as he dropped onto the edge of the sofa. His eyes were bloodshot with fatigue and the edges of his mouth turned down. "I can't let you do that. I failed you in Naples and he found us. Now more than ever, I've got to keep you safe."

"Then let's go after him and end this."

"No. We're not going anywhere. You'll stay here with me guarding you at all times."

Pride and the need for independence shot her temper from *fuming* right to *seriously pissed off.* "I really resent your dictating to me again, no matter how noble your intentions—"

"If you don't cooperate, I'll have you placed in protective custody." Emelio stood up; his normally melodic voice so ominous as to be almost unrecognizable. "I won't let another woman I—I'm responsible for get killed."

"What are you talking about, Emelio?"

Stevie was hell-bent on going after Braga. That was the last thing he could allow to happen. He was tired, so damn tired, but he had to gather enough energy to fight with her once more. He'd do whatever it took, including bare his soul, in order to make her understand that her safety was all that mattered now.

He stuffed both hands into his back pockets and took a deep breath. "Lina, the woman I told you I was involved with, was killed during a drug bust."

"She was a cop?"

"No. She was my informant."

Stevie's expression remained neutral for a moment, but he could see the wheels turning. Then her eyes narrowed beneath her golden eyebrows and her mouth flattened into a line of displeasure. "Please tell me I'm wrong about what I'm thinking. Tell me you didn't take this woman's virginity to get information."

"No!" Emelio recoiled at the implication, stung that she would even think it of him. "It wasn't like that."

"What was it like, then?"

"I'd just been transferred to the Special Operations Division from the Bureau. My first major undercover assignment was to find proof that Braga was using the *Viajes Caribe* travel agency for illegal fund transfers." He paused. "I was supposed to get the owner to trust me, get whatever evidence I could to further the case against the cartel."

Stevie turned away, her arms crossed under her breasts as she paced the room in long strides. "You said you had a relationship."

Emelio was quiet for a moment, remembering. "I cared for her, I admit it. Lina was young and very sweet and I believed in her innocence. Because of that, I wasn't thinking with my head."

"Not the one on your shoulders, anyway," Stevie muttered. When he shot her a dark look, her mouth twisted into a frown, but she apologized before asking, "What went wrong?"

So many things had gone wrong. Where the hell did he begin? He raked one hand through his hair. "I screwed up. Is that what you want to hear? I screwed up!"

"How?" Stevie paused near the balcony door, the humid breeze ruffling her hair.

Emelio sighed heavily and stared unseeingly at the floor, looking inward. "I was gone a lot and couldn't always explain, so Lina thought I was seeing another woman. She tried to follow me a couple of times. One day I wasn't careful enough. She saw me going into the Dade County Courthouse to testify in another case. Later, when she confronted me, I denied it, of course—"

"But the damage had been done." Her voice was flat, matter-of-fact. "I take it she refused to help you."

"Not directly. That would have been better for all of us. Like I said, I trusted in her innocence and in her love. I didn't count on the depth of her loyalty to Braga."

"You totally compromised your investigation."

Her tone was coolly impersonal, and he looked up to see judgment evident in her gaze. There was suddenly more than physical distance between them, and he knew that he'd disappointed her. His shoulders slumped, exhaustion and guilt weighing on him equally.

"It was the greatest lapse in judgment of my career. The cartel used the charter flights Lina booked to move cash out of the U.S. I warned her that she'd lose the agency, that I'd charge her as an accessory and send her to jail."

"You threatened her?"

"I did my job." His temper flared defensively. "The Special Operations Division was dying to get their hands on the cartel. Lina was an informant and the case had to come first."

An odd expression crossed her face. "The job has to take priority, doesn't it?"

"It should have, but things are never simply black-and-white." He massaged his temples with an unsteady hand, his voice shaking with self-disgust.

Emelio sat back down on the arm of the sofa. Old guilt and new combined to open a wound that had never really healed. What he'd done was unprofessional, unforgivable, and Lina had paid the ultimate price for his mistake.

"I confided in Alex, told him how it had all gone wrong. He put Lina under twenty-four-hour surveillance, but she still managed to contact her cousin."

Stevie stopped in front of him. "Her cousin?"

"Braga."

Her expression reflected utter disbelief then she glared at him. Both hands curled into fists. Her voice rose in accusation as she gave him a hard shove. "Damn you, Emelio. Damn you for lying to me!"

"What are you talking about?" He caught himself before he rolled backward off the sofa arm.

"You've known all along why Braga targeted me!"

His eyebrows drew together in a frown. "I didn't know anything about the meeting—"

Stevie stabbed her index finger toward him. "Oh,

come on! It never occurred to you that all of this was because of what you did?"

"Of course I thought Braga was trying to get back at me." He pushed himself off the couch and got to his feet. "I got inside the cartel, helped to seize millions in assets and disrupt their business. But there's no way I could have known he would come after you."

"You knew Lina was Braga's cousin. You slept with her and then turned her into an informant against him—"

"He's the one who set her up with the laundering business in the first place. How could that possibly be related to you?" His thoughts were drifting like fog through his brain. Extreme fatigue was preventing him from making sense of things.

Stevie shook her head, as if he was missing some important point. She clasped her fingers together, visibly trying to maintain control. "I'm an intelligent woman. I'm perfectly capable of making my own choices and decisions. Yet you don't trust me at all, do you?"

"That's not it, Stephanie." He reached for her, but she jerked her arm away. Though he understood, her rejection still hurt. "Lina accused me of using her, just like Braga did, and she was right. I was responsible for her, both personally and professionally. But she lost her life and my career at Justice was finished."

He'd been carrying a deep sense of failure and the heavy burden of responsibility ever since. Guilt made him unsure of himself, made him second-guess his decisions. He wanted so badly to regain his honor, but wasn't certain it was even possible after what he'd done.

Stevie's eyes were the color of the deepest part of a cresting wave, where dark blue riptides build. "This is your chance to make things right. Not just for Lina, but for your sake as well. Weston is weak. We'll confront him with the videotape and get him to help us get Braga."

Emelio rubbed his eyes, trying to get rid of the dull headache pounding behind them. She hadn't heard a word he said. Not about the danger or about her safety, not about his determination to protect her. None of it.

"We're not confronting anybody. We have got to take this slowly and do a thorough investigation. I want to make sure that Braga can't get off this time. That we take Weston down with him. And I want to make sure you live through it."

Stevie cursed softly under her breath, frustration igniting her temper again. Why wouldn't he understand that she couldn't sit around wringing her hands? This wasn't just a matter of control; it was a matter of survival.

"Just how long am I supposed to hide? I don't want to spend the rest of my life running. If Braga found us once, he can find us again. Let's turn the tables and go after him."

Emelio shook his head emphatically. "No, I can't let you—"

"Why won't you believe that I can handle this?"

"Your idea of handling this is right out of one of your movies. You're strong, you're smart. You're the most incredible woman I've ever met. But you've still got a lot to learn. Rules and procedures ensure convictions. You can't break or ignore them when someone's life is at stake. I learned that the hard way, but you don't have to."

Though his words were without malice, they still cut. She turned away to avoid his eyes. He was questioning her ability again and, after getting hurt last night, she supposed he had every right to. All along she'd been bragging about her classes, but when she had the chance to put theory into practice... Embarrassment burned color onto her cheeks while an old, too familiar sense of inadequacy tightened her chest.

"I promised to keep you safe, Stephanie. That means keeping you as far away from Braga as possible. He's ruthless enough to embroil an innocent young girl in his business, to put her in the line of fire. What do you think he'll do to someone who can connect him with the State's Attorney's Office?"

Stevie didn't answer, her attention caught by the television screen. The current news story was about the White Orchid Affair, a charity ball being held this evening. After the station went to commercial, she snapped off the set and focused on him.

"I'm sorry, Emelio. I know you're trying to do what you think is right. I just feel so helpless and I hate that."

He sighed and the tension between them eased. "I'm sorry too, but it has to be this way. No one outside of the SOD knows about this apartment so we should be safe for a while longer." Emelio yawned hugely. "Listen, I'm not sharp enough right now. Give me an hour, will you? Then wake me up and I'll arrange a search for that videotape."

He would arrange to get the video. Which meant they weren't going after it themselves. It had been hard enough being stuck in the cottage in Naples. She'd go crazy in this tiny apartment.

Her reluctance must have shown on her face because he held out his hand in invitation and in truce.

"I know you think I'm being unreasonable, Stephanie. But, now that we've found each other, I don't want to lose you."

"I know that. I feel the same way and I understand."

She returned his embrace, felt the heat of his body and the beating of his heart against her cheek. Sadly, she really did understand. Emelio was trying so hard not to repeat the past that he was making yet another mistake. But she wasn't going to argue with him anymore.

When she stepped back, Stevie saw that he was beyond tired. His eyes were dull and his face looked gaunt. Despite the resentment still simmering just below the surface, she was concerned about him. "You don't look like you can go another five minutes without sleep."

"Yeah. I'm pretty beat." He readily accepted the arm she slid around his waist as she walked with him to the bedroom.

"Get some rest, chér. Things will look a lot different when you wake up." She was careful not to make him suspicious, but something about that last news brief had sparked a memory and she planned to follow up on it without his interference.

Emelio didn't bother removing his clothes before flopping facedown on the bed. Stevie lay down beside him, one hand soothing his back. His head no more than touched the pillow before he fell into an exhaυsted slumber. She waited a few minutes just to be sure he didn't rouse.

She'd trusted him with her secrets and her heart. Yet Emelio had kept vital information from her all along. He'd mentioned an informant and a relationship, but hadn't told her the connection. Men could be so dense about emotional matters. Braga's need to avenge Lina was blatantly obvious to her.

The gleam on Emelio's silver armor had been tarnished in her eyes. She was all for zealously working a case, but sleeping with an informant crossed the line. It was childish of her to feel as if he'd somehow let her down, but there it was.

Last night on the beach had been a less than stellar display of her skills, but she had the means to put Braga and Weston behind bars and she fully intended to do so. Damned if she'd spend the rest of her life looking over one shoulder.

As Emelio snored softly into the pillow, she eased off the bed and found her shoes. A sense of loss settled heavily in her chest as she gazed at his sleeping features. Their newfound relationship would end once he realized she'd gone. Controlling men never liked it when a woman stood up for herself, especially not controlling men with good intentions.

Stevie loved him so much. But perhaps that love had been doomed from the start. She was too independent and Emelio was too protective. Going after Braga was something she had to do—it was the only way to protect the future. Someday Emelio might be a part of it again, but she didn't think so.

Out in the living room, she hunted for his keys. After a couple of minutes, though, she gave up. They must still be in the pocket of his jeans. She'd have to do it the hard way.

Stevie grabbed her cell phone off the desk, dropping it into her purse. As she started to close it, the picture in the side pocket caught her eye. It was the photo from the movie set, the one Tiffnee had grabbed… Oh, no. Tiffnee had taken the picture *before* Emelio ever saw it.

She looked in the direction of the bedroom, uncertain of what to do. Emelio hadn't lied to her. He didn't know what Braga had seen in the picture, what the expression on his face revealed. Stevie huffed out a breath, shaking her head at this further complication. Maybe she should stay, wait for him to wake up and apologize.

But if she stayed, she'd lose precious time. She needed to act now, while Braga still thought he had them cornered. The White Orchid Ball was tonight and she had a lot to do before then. She pulled the photograph from her purse, torturing herself with the image of Emelio's smoldering gaze.

That picture represented all that might have been possible. She left it on the sofa for him to find later. Then she walked out of the apartment, scrubbing at the tears on her cheeks as she stumbled down the stairs. She had to make the right choice for both of them. That meant making Braga pay for everything he'd done.

Stevie looked both ways on the sidewalk to make sure no one was watching. Grateful the Jeep window was partially open, she reached inside to pop the door lock and slide into the driver's seat. After making sure the gearshift was in neutral, she casually reached beneath the steering column. Then she grabbed the pair of red wires and crossed them, just as Emelio had taught her.

The Jeep rumbled to life and she started to pull away from the curb when something occurred to her. Stevie got out and crouched down to feel under the passenger-side wheel well, just as Emelio had back in the parking garage in Miami. There, as she suspected, was a magnetic box with a spare set of keys. Good thing. She hadn't looked forward to hot-wiring a stolen vehicle at the next gas station.

There was an awful grinding noise when she tried to shove the shifter into first gear. She'd confused the clutch and the brake. Finally, she got the hang of a manual transmission and, after a couple of wrong turns, found her way back to I-95. Once on the interstate, she settled in for the seventy-mile drive to the Stockton estate.

11

AN HOUR AND A HALF LATER, Stevie turned onto Southern Boulevard and drove across Lake Worth onto the island of Palm Beach. Cruising along scenic South Ocean Boulevard, a low seawall separated the road from the champagne-colored sand on her right. On the left, palm trees and fifteen-foot hedges shielded the opulent estates from gaping tourists like her.

She pulled up to the gates of the Stockton compound, a European-style mansion with Italianate towers silhouetted against the pale blue sky. After a brief wait, a male, British-accented voice came over the intercom. "Yes? May I help you?"

"It's Stephanie Madison from January Investigations. I'm here to check on a problem with the security cameras."

"So sorry, but the Stocktons have flown to Bermuda for the weekend."

Stevie grinned. This was going to be easier than she thought. She injected a note of outrage into her voice and pretended not to remember the good-looking, twentysomething Englishman. "Who are you? What are you doing here?"

The young Brit sputtered for a few seconds then responded with a little indignation of his own. "I am Maxwell, the Stockton's butler and personal chef."

"Not for long, Max. You've breached the safety measures by telling me your employers' whereabouts. What if I were a thief casing the joint so I could rob it later? The Stocktons won't be happy to find out how free you are with their information."

An almost tangibly embarrassed silence followed. Stevie drummed her fingers on the Jeep's door frame and frowned. Was he going for it or not?

"Listen, Max. We met back in December when I installed the new security cameras. I got a call saying there was some kind of malfunction so I need to do a systems check. On a beautiful Saturday afternoon, no less. So how about letting me in?"

Still he hesitated. "I don't suppose I could persuade you not to inform my employers about all of this?"

She considered it for a second. If she promised to stay quiet, the butler might be more cooperative. But she couldn't do it. She took her job and her clients' safety too seriously to overlook the situation. "Sorry. There's no way."

A heavy sigh sounded over the intercom. "Just as well, really. I'd been thinking of giving notice."

"Don't worry, Max. Who wouldn't want a personal chef? I could use some lunch myself."

One hour and one hundred videotapes later, Stevie sat in the basement-level control room nibbling on the spinach-and-wild-mushroom ravioli Maxwell had whipped up for her.

Each of the cameras she'd installed had motion sensors and therefore only recorded when someone entered the room. It was a tedious process to check the actual contents against the label. The videos had been marked with the name of the room, but not any specific dates. At the moment she was reviewing footage from one of the upstairs bedrooms, namely the maid going in to take care of the room and then of Mr. Stockton going in to take care of the maid.

There it was! Stevie dropped her fork and jerked forward. She finally saw what she was looking for—Jack Weston walking in just ahead of Rogelio Braga. And the hidden camera's microphone had picked up their conversation.

"I'm sorry, Señor Braga, but it's not that easy. I'm taking a considerable risk—"

"*No me vengas con tus pendejadas.*" Braga's tone was sharp and menacing.

"Um, excuse me?"

"I said, do not bother me with your bloody stupid problems. You are well aware I am not a man who easily forgives a debt."

Weston seemed to pale as he shifted from one foot to the other. Stevie thought she heard him swallow hard on the audio recording. Then Braga spoke again.

"Your habit of betting on the wrong horses at Hialeah Park cannot be overlooked. Nor would the authorities ignore your other habit of accepting bribes to cover your losses."

Weston bowed his head, his mouth drawn into the kind of frown worn by men who know they're trapped.

"If you wish to clear your obligation to me, these two matters must be handled immediately. Failure will have unfortunate consequences."

"Yes, sir. I'll take care of it." Weston reluctantly offered his hand. Braga reached for it and, by the look on the Assistant State's Attorney's face, squeezed too hard. The door to the room swung wide just as Braga said, "Until the White Orchid then."

Then Stevie saw herself in the drab-looking guard uniform she'd been forced to wear that night. She listened to her own voice saying, *"I'm sorry, gentlemen, but the upstairs of the house is off-limits to guests,"* before stopping the tape.

She had them!

Or did she? Stevie replayed the segment of the tape, concentrating on the exact words. Weston obviously owed Braga, but there was no way to know how he was paying off the debt. Shit. It wasn't enough.

The video certainly implicated Weston in illegal conduct; these two men had no rational excuse for being seen together. But Braga hadn't said anything specific that could be used against him. She'd have to gamble that she was right about where they would be tonight.

Stevie found a blank tape and prepared a copy of the video segment while she came up with a plan of action.

IT WAS AMAZING how quickly rage could wake a person up.

Emelio had slept longer than he'd intended, giving Stevie at least two hours head start. He had woken up with a sense that something was wrong. Alerted by the silence in the apartment, he'd wandered out to the living room to find Stevie long gone.

Damn good thing. He would never in his life strike a woman, but right now he might seriously consider throttling one.

She'd been so caring, so concerned while she

helped him to bed. Hell, she'd even rubbed his back. If he closed his eyes, he could still feel the tender warmth of her touch. Stupid! He'd fallen under her spell when all the while she'd set him up.

Had she even waited for him to fall asleep before stealing the Jeep and stranding him in Little Havana? The utter shock of it had burned away any residual fatigue, leaving him pissed off and edgy and alone in the empty apartment.

Maybe that was what he resented most. Here he was supposed to be the professional and yet he'd let an amateur fool him into letting down his guard. Even in his sleep-deprived state, he should have seen it coming. Stevie never gave in without a hell of a fight.

And that worried him more than anything else. Emelio pressed a hand against the glass pane of the balcony door, resting his forehead on his wrist. Tight knots formed in the muscles of his neck and shoulders. Where could Stevie have gone? He turned away from the door and suddenly focused on a photograph lying on the couch.

He walked over to pick it up and his heart constricted in his chest. *Madre de Dios.* His legs gave out and he sank onto the cushion. The close angle had perfectly captured Stevie's beautiful smile. Her slate-blue eyes glowed with amusement as she looked at something in the distance. He saw himself in the picture, as well, his gaze oblivious to anything but her.

His expression was openly admiring, unguarded and in love. Everything was right there on his face and he saw what Braga must have—the raw evidence of his feelings for Stevie. Emelio sank back against the couch, his left hand covering his eyes.

Now he understood why Stevie thought he'd lied to her. Anyone looking at that picture would have known how much he cared for her. Except that Emelio hadn't realized it himself, not until Naples. He'd had no idea his feelings were worn so blatantly on his sleeve. That was all his nemesis would have needed in order to plot revenge.

He leaped to his feet, raking his fingers through the tangles in his hair. In his mind's eye he saw Lina, covered in blood and reaching out to him, her eyes shimmering with pain just before the light faded away, etching her forever-accusing stare onto his memory.

He had to find Stevie. Now.

He figured she was trying to get the videotape from the client. After that, he had no idea where to look for her. He checked his front pockets for quarters and hiked down the steps to use the pay phone in the bodega. He needed to call Alex to break the news about the Jeep and to get a lift to the office.

Back upstairs, he went into the kitchenette and heated up the last of the café Cubano in hopes the caffeine would jump-start his brain. Stevie was smart enough not to return to her apartment, but she was also relentless. It would be just like her to ignore everything he'd said and go after Weston. His mind leaped from one possibility to the next, careening his emotions from anger to the kind of anxiety that rippled down his spine and left his whole body chilled. He closed his eyes, thinking hard…

The news!

The coffee turned to acid in his stomach as he set the mug down with a bang. She'd been watching that segment about the charity ball. There must be a connection between Braga and the White Orchid Affair. She had remembered something but chose to punish him instead of revealing what she knew. Damn that woman's stubbornness.

Stevie was walking into a viper's nest in a bid to prove something to him. And, more importantly, to herself. Her fierce need to be in control, to not be seen as a victim, could very well get her killed. Since he didn't know exactly what she had planned, he'd have to make some plans of his own.

For more than three years the SOD team had been united in their quest to bring down the Ramos cartel. These people had put everything, sometimes their careers and often their lives, on the line because they wanted justice and they wanted revenge.

Now, Emelio was going to ask them to do it again, but outside of channels. For a chance at Braga, he was sure they'd help him protect Stevie at the White Orchid Affair.

Madre de Dios, just let him find her in time.

FIVE MILES FROM downtown Miami, across the Rickenbacker Causeway, the Smith-Carlyle Key Biscayne rose majestically from twelve acres of tropical gardens bordered by oceanfront vistas. The barrier-island resort, built to rival the finest European hotels, was discreetly pleased to count both royalty and rock stars among their return guests.

Stevie parked the Jeep between a stretch limousine and a vintage Bentley under the port-coche. After meeting the valet's smirk with a disdainfully raised eyebrow, she swept past him to the entrance. Admiring the West Indies colonial decor in passing, she sauntered through the lobby with nothing more than her purse and an attitude.

"Hi. Stephanie Madison."

The desk clerk greeted her with a sympathetic nod. "Of course, Ms. Madison. We have your reservation. I'm terribly sorry about the situation with the airline. I'll have your luggage sent up as soon as it arrives."

"Thank you." She slid a platinum credit card across the desk, grateful that her credit limit had never been reduced after the divorce. "In the meantime, can you arrange for someone at Neiman Marcus to bring over a selection of white evening gowns with matching footwear?"

"Certainly. Size…?"

"Ten. And size nine for the shoes." Stevie gave the clerk a smile, fluttering her eyelashes. "Thank you very much."

Entering her executive-level suite, Stevie's heels sank into the plush jade-green carpet. Framed lithographs decorated walls papered in pale mint-and-white pinstripe. Richly upholstered dark wood furniture graced the living room and ceramic pots of flowering jasmine scented the air.

A set of ornate French doors led to a generously appointed bedroom. Luxurious cream-colored linens and goose-down pillows invited her to snuggle onto the king-size bed. Her thoughts turned to Emelio, imagining them bringing one of the black-lace letters to life in this gorgeous room.

That was never going to happen, though, not now. If he was even awake yet, he would be furious. Stevie shook off the weight of her regret. She had work to do. After tipping the bellboy, she secured her copy of the Stockton videotape in the bedroom safe.

Then she kicked off her shoes and padded barefoot to the wide glass sliders. The balcony view of Biscayne Bay ten stories below was spectacular. Seagulls wheeled through the air above cigarette boats slicing through the channel. She left the doors open, allowing a sultry breeze to billow through the floral draperies.

Stevie walked over to the antique secretary and picked up the room-service menu. After perusing the many choices of gourmet cuisine, she dialed the kitchen to place an order for a very late lunch. "This is room 1017. I'd like a hamburger, medium rare, with Colby cheese, mustard, mushrooms, lettuce and tomato. And also a large order of fries."

She created a script in her head while she ate. Every good poker player knows that in order to bluff, you have to believe. Stevie wasn't that great at cards but she figured she'd watched enough spy movies to pull off a decent con.

She used the hotel phone to track down the Assistant State's Attorney, finally interrupting his family barbecue. Her pulse leaped with apprehension when he came on the line. She swallowed hard and prepared to show her hand.

"Jack Weston." His voice was a little thick, probably from too much hot sun and cold beer.

"Hello, Mr. Weston. You're in one hell of a lot of trouble." She kept her tone light and cheerful, the telemarketer of his nightmares.

"Who is this?" he demanded.

"Stevie Madison."

She sensed his recognition and alarm, but he tried to pretend otherwise. "Madison…? Madison…"

Because of him, she'd been forced to run. She'd been in hiding all week. Seething resentment gave her voice an edge before she could control it. "You want to play games, or do you want me to tell you what I know?"

"I have no idea what you're talking about—"

She cut him off, suddenly impatient with his evasion. "I saw you with Braga at the Stockton's holiday party."

A grave silence came over the phone line. She couldn't even hear him breathing. When Weston finally spoke, his voice was devoid of inflection. "You're crazy."

"You wish." Stevie's laugh was tainted with derision as she stared down at the late-afternoon sun glimmering on the blue waters of the Bay.

"Are you recording this nonsense? Because I warn you—"

"Relax, Jack, I'm on a cell phone. You're pretty good with cell phones, aren't you? Like I said, I saw you shake hands with Rogelio Braga. That's not the kind of thing that will advance your career."

The slurring of his words betrayed Weston's feeble attempt at disbelief. "I don't recall exactly—"

"I thought we weren't going to play games?" Stevie turned away from the windows and paced across the room. "I'm prepared to go public unless we make a deal."

"How can I be sure you haven't gone to anyone with these lies already?"

"You can't, Jack."

Weston's chuckle was humorless. "How much do you want?"

She hesitated, momentarily stunned by the twist in the conversation. Maybe she wasn't the only one trying to bluff. "How do I know you're not the one recording this?"

"Ten thousand dollars."

Stevie snorted, as though he'd insulted her, but she had to be careful not to cross the line to extortion. She was already on shaky ground for the blackmail.

Weston kept talking. "Yeah, you look like the high-maintenance type. Thirty."

Then again, he's the one who brought up the money. "Come on, Jack. My information is worth more than that."

"Today's Saturday. The banks are closed."

"Remind me to be sympathetic."

Weston sighed dramatically. "Fifty? Fifty thousand is a lot of money. It could take me a while."

Her reply dripped sarcasm. "I'm sure Braga can loan you some cash."

Another silence greeted her. It was time to give him a push in the direction she wanted him to go. "You don't think your career is worth that much? How about your life?"

"I guess we should meet to discuss this in person." Weston sounded resigned.

"Fine. I'll see you tonight."

"Tonight?" She'd surprised him at last. "But—"

Stevie hung up the phone and exhaled in a slow whoosh. The stress eased from her shoulders even as another emotion swelled in her chest. Pride. This was going to work. She'd found a way to take Weston and Braga down. She felt empowered, completely in control for the first time in too long. She'd made her own decisions and handled things on her own terms.

Wait until she told Emelio…

Actually, it would have to wait. She hadn't seen a

telephone in the apartment in Little Havana and she didn't know if Emelio still had his mobile. The only way to contact him would be through the agency, if anyone was even working in the office today. After digging out her cell phone, she pressed the send button to call the most recently dialed number.

"STEVIE."

Emelio jerked his head up when his partner answered the phone. "Where is she?"

Alex cupped his palm over the mouthpiece and whispered, "She's at the Carlyle."

He closed his eyes briefly, relief washing over and through him at the knowledge she was still alive.

"Why would you contact Weston?" Alex narrowed his eyes in a disgruntled expression. "No, explain it to me now. I'd like to know what the hell is going on."

Emelio's reaction was a single vicious curse. Stevie had tipped their hand to the target. She'd taken a precarious situation, doused it in gasoline and lit the fuse so there was no way to avoid an explosive confrontation. And yet, beneath the surface, was a reluctant admiration. In her determination to take control of her life, Stevie had turned the hunter into the prey and altered all the rules of the game.

"If you live through this, I'll probably have to fire you." Alex sighed heavily. "In the meantime, stay at the hotel. Don't do anything else until I get there. What? Don't even—"

Emelio gave him a quizzical look, wondering what Stevie had said before she hung up on Alex.

His best friend and partner gave him a wry glance. "She's going shopping."

HIGH-TECH HARDWARE WAS deliberately hard to find, located in a nondescript building with reflective windows that were actually two-way mirrors. No signs were evident anywhere and Bernie Sevel took no pains to advertise. If you didn't know where his business was, he wasn't going to help you find him.

Bernie sold "covert communications products" out of a storefront in North Miami. Stevie walked up to the front door, pressed the bell and waved at the security camera that whirred as it captured her image. A long beep sounded and the electronic locks disengaged to allow her to open the door.

"Hey, little girl! How ya been?"

"I'm doing good, Bernie."

The burly ex-New York City cop greeted her from the other side of a steel cage. The thick bars limited access to the gadgets and guns lining the shelves until Bernie determined whether he wanted a customer's business. She braced for impact as he came from behind the counter to give her a bear hug.

The black T-shirt stretched across his massive chest was emblazoned with the slogan, *In God We Trust. Everybody Else Gets Monitored.* Sevel Elite Security had trained her in Advanced Executive Protection and Bernie himself had taught her Martial Arts for Bodyguards class.

"Great ta see you, Stevie. What ya up to these days?"

"I'm still in the investigation business, working my first undercover assignment."

"Told ya." A proud grin split his weathered features. "I told ya you'd do it someday. You were one of my best students."

"Thanks, Bernie." Stevie looked around at row after row of items such as sniper rifles, infrared illumination, bomb detectors and telephonic voice changers. ''I need to pick out some of your toys.''

Bushy gray brows crinkled into a mock scowl. ''This is high-quality, cutting-edge stuff, little girl. I don't sell no toys.''

Stevie smiled briefly. ''Good thing, because I'm not playing. This case is as serious as it gets. The guy came after me personally, so I've got to take him down.''

Bernie scratched his snowy buzz cut and eyed her dubiously. ''You ain't going after him alone, I hope?''

She swallowed her instinctive resentment. It seemed as if blue-eyed blondes were never taken seriously and she was damned sick of being patted on the head. But she needed her former instructor's guidance. ''No, Bernie, of course not. The team just wants a few equalizers.''

He nodded sagely. ''Okay, doll. Tell me what ya need.''

THE WHITE, LIQUID SATIN Armani gown had significantly increased Stevie's credit card debt.

However, the narrow straps and square bodice showcased her cleavage while the loose, flowing skirt with its off-center split allowed for unrestricted movement. Wide elastic garters held her sheer thigh-high stockings in place and matched the lace of her white panties.

She wrestled her short hair into a riot of golden curls and swept shadow across her eyes the way she'd seen her mother do every day of her childhood. As she replaced the plain gold-hoop earrings with cascades of cubic zirconium, her vision clouded and she saw another woman in another mirror.

"Stephanie! You'll ruin Mommy's face!"

The little girl, sweetly dressed in pink and frills, bit her lip and her small fingers dropped away from her mother's cheek. "I just wanted to give you a kiss."

"Not now, princess. I'm late as it is." Frown lines cut between her perfectly arched brows, marring the beautifully remote expression.

"Can you tuck me in first?"

"Mrs. Singleton will put you to bed. I'll see you in the morning."

The little girl fixed her gaze on their reflections, afraid to look directly at the grown woman she tried so hard to emulate, afraid to anger her with the tears trembling on her lashes. "I love you, Mama."

Her mother turned away, anxious to leave. "Be a good girl, Stephanie, and do as you're told."

Stevie closed her eyes, blocking the memory and the rush of sorrow that lodged in her throat. She'd been a good girl, done everything her parents expected and look what it had gotten her.

Not wanting to dwell on painful memories, she instead practiced the line of reasoning she planned to make to Alex. Studying her facial expressions in the mirror, she made certain her appearance remained neutral, not defensive nor desperate.

Her future was in jeopardy. This was not only her first undercover mission, but also the chance to prove herself once and for all. In the back of her mind, however, she knew there was much more at stake than just her credibility.

A knock at the front door startled her out of her reverie. Alex was here. Was he with her backup team or the guys who would take charge? It would depend on how well she presented her argument. Either way, she had no intention of sitting on the sidelines.

She walked across the suite, each step increasing the nervous flutter in her belly. Taking a deep calming breath, she swung the door wide and came face to face with…

"Emelio!"

12

A RUSH OF FEAR AND ADRENALINE hit Stevie's system before she could control her reaction.

Although Emelio looked gorgeous dressed in a jet-black business suit, the snowy linen of his shirt contrasting the golden hue of his skin, he also looked furious. His rich brown hair was combed back from his forehead, emphasizing amber-green eyes that once again held her at a distance.

His accusing stare bored into hers, and she had to fight the urge to start babbling apologies and explanations. He wasn't her ex-husband and she hadn't done anything wrong. Well, maybe she could have handled things differently, but she stood by her decision to get the videotape. Still, she was at a complete loss for what to say in the face of his anger.

Their standoff was broken by a wolf whistle. "Very nice."

Stevie's gaze darted behind Emelio to see Alex, two guys from the agency and two other men she didn't know. One of her colleagues, Jason Knight, wore a waiter's outfit, with a small brass name tag falsely proclaiming him a member of hotel staff, and a huge grin.

She stood back to let the men inside, sweeping her arm with a flourish and stifling the unwarranted hurt when Emelio brushed past her without a word. "Glad you like it, Jase. I'm going to bill the agency for reimbursement.''

''I wasn't talking about the suite, hot stuff.''

Emelio turned his head and shot Jason a piercing glare. He seemed about to make some kind of remark when Alex clapped a hand on his shoulder. ''Lighten up, hombre.''

She followed the group into the living room, addressing Alex since he was the safer of her two choices. ''You're not planning to wear that downstairs, are you?''

He affected an insulted expression as he glanced down at his purple, blue and yellow Hawaiian-print shirt. ''What are you talking about? This is one of my fav—''

''Can we get this party started?'' Emelio's interruption was terse, both a question and a command. He stood in the middle of the room, arms crossed tightly over his chest. His eyes looked everywhere but at her.

Stevie clenched her fingers together behind her back to keep her hands from shaking as she filled the awkward silence with bright chatter. ''So, the gang's all here. I know Jason and Rick obviously. But who are the two mystery guests?''

Though she directed her question to Emelio, hoping to connect, hoping to breach the weighted silence, it was Alex who answered. ''This is David Heintz of the FBI and Oscar Solis from the DEA. We worked together in the SOD.''

''Hi. I'm GTMY.'' Stevie nodded to each man. A faint blush colored her cheeks when they all stared at her, confused. ''Um, glad to meet you. I was just trying to fit in.''

When the chuckles died away, Oscar Solis cleared his throat and settled into one of the wing chairs. ''Just so we're all crystal clear about the situation, the Justice Department is taking charge. Once Ms. Madison tells us what she knows, we'll run with the ball.''

''Wait a minute. I thought—''

Solis cut her off. ''For years, Braga has managed to stay just out of reach. If we don't get solid evidence that he's screwed with the court system, our three-year joint effort will be for nothing.''

''Besides,'' Alex said quietly, ''as private investigators, we don't have arrest authority.''

Her eyebrows creased in displeasure. All of these guys had worked on some aspect of the Ramos case, leaving her the unwanted girl in the old boys' club. They didn't come here to help her. They came to take over, just as she'd suspected. Her temper flared and she glanced at Emelio.

He finally looked at her and she found herself wishing he hadn't. She practically melted from the heat radiating across the ten feet that separated them, but she met his scowl with both apology and defiance.

Emelio's voice was carefully neutral while he suggested the team go over the hotel blueprints and break out the equipment they'd brought with them. Then he looked at Stevie and cocked his head to one side. ''I need to speak with you a moment.''

He moved across the room before she could blink. His arm was like a steel band behind her back as he ''escorted'' her away from the others. Once in the bedroom, Emelio slammed the French doors, cutting off her escape.

Tension rolled off him in waves, and, despite his effort to keep control, his eyes were no longer cold.

Emotions flashed across his features too quickly for her to name, but there was no doubt he was upset.

Stevie wrapped her arms over her waist and shifted from one foot to the other. This was going to be rough and she braced herself for a nasty argument. He remained silent, however, simply looking her up and down with an unfathomable gaze. She cleared her throat, hoping to head off the explosion.

"I know you're angry, Emelio, and I'm sorry for ditching you like—"

She flinched when he grabbed her by the shoulders. Then he dropped his head and his lips prevented any more words. He slanted his mouth over hers hungrily, ravishing her. How in heaven's name was it possible for a kiss to be punishing and tender at the same time?

Stevie stopped wondering and simply lost herself in his embrace. His tongue designed sensual patterns in the warmth of her mouth while his hands, his hands were everywhere at once. His touch was soft yet possessive as his fingers stroked her cheek, her bare shoulders, her back.

It was all there, every emotion he'd hidden in front of the team was right there in that kiss. The sense of connection returned, hot and insistent, with the power to erase the past, if only for a moment. The rush of longing and need hit her so hard she was shaking as Emelio devoured her lips in a kiss that should have set them both aflame.

Then he cupped her face between his palms and gently pulled back. She held him tightly, inhaling the citrus spice of his aftershave. They stood, foreheads touching, breathing rushed, until she felt him move away. Stevie raised her lashes to look at him.

No longer turbulent, his eyes were instead filled

with heartbreaking tenderness. Her heart rejoiced. They would get through this, they would take Braga down and then see what the future held for them. Every time she looked at him, the love she felt intensified. Especially now, when he had every right to castigate her for going off alone, but instead kissed her as if his life depended on it.

Maybe now wasn't the best time to tell him how she felt, not with a criminal to catch and a handful of agents in the next room, but the declaration was on the tip of her tongue. That is, until he moved toward the dresser and reached for a tissue. He wiped her kiss from his lips, and, when he turned back to face her, Mr. Calm, Cool and Controlled had returned.

"I need to know exactly everything you've done since flying off on your own so I can assess the damage to this operation." He tossed the lipstick-stained tissue into the trash can.

Emelio may as well have slapped her.

"The case? You want to talk about the case. Right now?"

Stevie stared at him in disbelief. He had turned her into a quivering mass of hormones and then shut himself off like a switch. She was so stunned she couldn't even identify her emotions—too many of them were vying for precedence. "What the hell was that?"

"Your call to Weston may have blown this investigation—"

"Was that kiss some kind of demonstration? Show the little woman who's boss? What the hell *was* that?"

Emelio finally met her gaze. His eyes glowed with sparks of golden fire, rocking her to the core and adding to her confusion. "That was me, damn glad to see you're all right."

Sincerity was evident in the timbre of his voice, in the expression on his face. She fought to make sense of the contradictory feelings arcing between them as desire warred with aggravation.

"You're making me nuts, you know that?"

"Join the club, lady. I've been going crazy with worry about you."

"Hey, you're the one who said an investigation has to take priority." She wasn't quite ready to declare a truce. "I followed my instincts about that videotape. I couldn't live with myself if I didn't do what I thought was right."

Emelio rubbed his forehead, the epitome of exasperation. "Neither can I, Stephanie. You're my responsibility. It's my job to keep you safe—"

"I don't want to be a responsibility, Emelio. I want to be…something more." Stevie twisted her fingers together, suddenly unsure she wanted to voice her true wish.

"You already are, believe me. And when all of this is over, we have unfinished business." He slipped his hand inside the lapel of his jacket and showed her black-lace letter number nine. "We have a lot to talk about, you and I. But, right now, we need to get back to the team and figure out how we're going to salvage the investigation."

Stevie turned and went to the wall safe. After disengaging the lock, she pulled out the Stockton tape.

Emelio frowned at the videocassette. "This should have been handled according to specific procedure. I told you, we have to do things by the book in order to ensure a conviction."

"Sometimes you have to throw out the rule book, Emelio. You guys wouldn't be here right now if not for the way I got things done." She stalked over to the French doors, yanking them open.

Jason blanched, pretending he hadn't been listening at the door and Stevie pretended not to notice. The other men looked up from the equipment and settled into chairs as Special Agent Solis turned to her expectantly.

"So, Stevie. Alex here gave us an overview, but we need you to fill in the specifics of your little chat with Weston."

She briefly explained how she'd connected Braga to the White Orchid through the news brief and then confirmed it with the videotape. Then she told them about her conversation with Weston. Alex and Solis glanced at each other while the other men shuffled in their seats, making her feel embarrassed and defensive.

She propped the videotape on her hip and frowned at them. "What?"

Agent Heintz spoke up. "Does the term 'entrapment' mean anything to you? A good lawyer will get anything Weston said thrown out of court."

"You know as well as I do, a private citizen can't entrap a criminal unless they're working for the government. I was investigating an agency case, not helping the Justice Department."

"Coercion is still not an acceptable method of evidence gathering, Ms. Madison."

"I didn't coerce him. I simply furnished him with the opportunity to commit a crime. Weston is the one who first mentioned a payoff, so that's all the proof we need to show that he's predisposed to criminal activity. A good lawyer will get our evidence right back in."

Stevie paused when she noticed Emelio's bemused expression. "I forgot to tell you. One of my classes was Introduction to Criminal Law."

Special Agent Solis cleared his throat. "All the same, Stevie—"

Alex held up both palms in a bid for peace. "Let's work the problem, and leave the rest for the courts."

"You want Braga. You're going to get him." Stevie walked over to the entertainment center and switched on the television set. The room fell silent as they all watched Braga and Weston on the screen.

"If you wish to clear your obligation to me, these two matters must be handled immediately."

"Yes, sir. I'll take care of it."

"Until the White Orchid then."

Stevie clicked the remote control to stop the tape. "I think you'll agree that the ends justify the means."

Solis nodded in approval, his only acknowledgment of her success. "All right, gentlemen. Here's how we're going to proceed."

"Wait a minute," Alex interrupted. "Do we have confirmation that Weston is actually here?"

She tried to answer. "If we check—"

Jason jumped in with a question. "What about the money issue? He knows Stevie is coming, so he'll be suspicious if she tries to nail him on the bribe."

"And what about a warrant?" Rick asked.

Heintz replied, "We can make a warrantless arrest since we've got more than reasonable grounds to believe Weston committed a felony."

"But we're going to need one to actually record from the transmitters we brought," Alex pointed out.

Solis agreed. ''Okay. I'll find a judge who's willing to accommodate us on a Saturday night. Let me take the video with me as proof.''

''That's fine,'' Stevie began. ''I left the original—''

Heintz cut her off again. ''We got the cooperation of hotel management for Emelio, Jason and Rick to pose as staff. Four more agents are en route...''

She might as well not even be here. As the men continued to discuss strategies and make plans, Stevie wandered over to the balcony. Old hurt and insecurities churned in her belly. She'd been shut out, despite the major contribution she'd made to the case, leaving her feeling condescended to and insignificant. She had no problem identifying her emotions right now—disappointed, frustrated and resentful.

Behind her, Rick clapped his hands together once. ''Okay, what's our next move?''

Emelio's voice rose above the others. ''That's for Stevie to decide.''

She swung around to look at him, eyebrows arched in surprise. Did she hear him correctly? The faces staring at Emelio mirrored her reaction. But his adamant expression dared anyone to question his decision.

''Stevie made the connection that's going to blow this investigation wide open. Let her run this part of the operation. She's earned the chance.''

She felt a warm glow spread through her body. Her lashes fluttered down to hide the effect his support had on her. She couldn't show her feelings in front of the men, but, inside, her heart swelled with elation. Despite the screwup on the beach and the way she'd left Little Havana, Emelio trusted her.

He trusted her.

Special Agent Solis reluctantly agreed to the idea. "All right, Ms. Madison. You've got your shot."

Emelio looked at her and in his eyes she saw that he understood all the things she couldn't say. The corners of his wide mouth tipped into a slight smile. "So, just how are you planning to get into this invitation-only, white-tie party?"

Excitement bubbled along her nerves and Stevie grinned mischievously. "I'm going to walk right through the front door."

FRANKIE RAMOS WAS DEAD. Long live Rogelio Braga.

It had not been easy to discover where Ramos was hiding and even more difficult to get his assassin into the room. But it had been well worth the money and the risk. The cartel was now completely under his command.

One problem had been eliminated and the other was about to be delivered to him like a saint's day gift. This Stevie Madison thought, correctly, that Weston was soft, and that he would pay for her silence. But Braga had something else in mind for Sanchez's woman.

Although Weston insisted that she had to be working alone because Sanchez always operated inside of the law, Braga knew otherwise. He might not break a law, but Sanchez had no compunction about bending the rules. After forcing Carolína into his bed, he'd terrorized her, promising to send her to jail as an accessory or deport her if she didn't betray her family.

Braga closed his eyes against the pain brought on by memory. Carolína, his sweet lovely Carolína…

Tonight, he would set another trap, using the Madison woman as bait to lure Sanchez out of hiding.

And this time, Braga would make sure there was no escape.

"MAY I SEE YOUR INVITATION, ma'am?"

A registration table had been set up in the foyer just off the main lobby of the hotel. All around Stevie, the cream of society mixed with the current political top bananas, making for a very elite charity dessert. It was hard to believe that a man like Braga could circulate among such a crowd without them ever guessing the true nature of his business.

A twinge of apprehension danced along her spine. She was about to con her way into "the" social event of the Miami season. She'd been given the chance to do real undercover work and she wanted to prove she was equal to the task. She wanted to make Emelio proud.

Emelio.

She pictured him sitting in the hotel manager's office, listening to the sound of her breathing through the hidden microphones in the earrings she'd bought at High-Tech Hardware. He was counting on her and she couldn't let him down. She ignored the twinge of uncertainty that tried to surface. She could do this.

The registrar was still waiting for her reply. He eyed her expectantly from behind wire-rimmed glasses. She gave him a haughty look in return, tilting her head just enough to peer down her nose at his receding hairline.

"I don't have my invitation."

"In that case, I'm afraid—"

"I am, however, on the guest list." She leaned one

hand on the desk and thrust her chest out, drawing his attention to the revealing neckline of her gown.

His puppy-brown eyes gave her cleavage an appreciative glance before he pasted on a politely dismissive expression. "Without an invitation, ma'am—"

"Check the guest list for Bill and Sigourney Madison. My husband wasn't able to attend at the last minute."

The registrar still looked skeptical, so she tried her mother's infamous "servant stare." It worked every time, especially on Stevie. She shoved the thought aside and said a prayer for her gamble. Every year, her parents paid a thousand dollars per ticket, whether they actually attended or not. She just hoped that this time they'd taken the tax write-off and stayed in New Orleans.

She heard Emelio's voice through the subvocal transceiver in her ear. "If there's a problem, walk away. Don't call any more attention to yourself. We'll find another way to get you inside."

There was no better way. She'd planned it out carefully and he would just have to give her more time. While the registrar ran a long, bony finger along the master list, she turned to the couple behind her. She didn't have to fake her annoyance when she spoke.

"Really, I must say something to Garnett Easley about this. It's a charity ball, for God's sake, not a summit meeting."

The patrician couple didn't reply, apparently not wanting to waste their breath on someone who was about to get thrown out of the White Orchid Affair on her Armani clad butt.

The anxiety returned. Even when she'd been part of this kind of crowd, she'd never belonged, never fit in. The uncomfortable reminder of her past made her long for a chilled chardonnay... She swallowed hard, dismayed by how easily she'd fallen toward her old crutch.

Stevie clenched her fingers a little tighter around her handbag. She had a job to do and a career to jump-start. If she was going to play, she might as well play it over the top. "Oh, look, there's Kryssie and Og. I didn't realize they were an item again after—Well, after what happened."

The couple shifted their attention from Her Royal Highness Maria Krystina of Greece and Baron Ogden von Erklentz back to Stevie with renewed interest. Her mother's addiction to society gossip paid off. After all, everybody who was anybody knew what had happened.

The registrar cleared his throat contritely. "My apologies, Mrs. Madison. Of course you're on the guest list. Please enjoy your evening."

"Good work, Jayne. You did it." Emelio's tone was somehow intimate, even though the whole SOD team was listening. The sound of his lightly accented voice sent warm ripples of pleasure along her nerves, calming her.

Pzzzt. Shhhh. His words were followed by a burst of static and Stevie tried not to wince. She brushed her hair forward on the right side and nodded regally, both acknowledging the registrar's apology and making sure the earpiece remained hidden. Then she strode along the corridor toward the entrance to the Grand Ballroom.

Beneath enormous crystal chandeliers, tables set with white linen, polished silver and glowing candelabra had been arranged along the gilded silk walls.

A cool Atlantic breeze drifted in through the open doors, gently rustling the pure white butterfly orchids and Casablanca lilies in their towering vases.

The murmur and hum of countless conversations echoed off the peach marble floor, almost drowning out the music. This year the theme of the ball was Winterfest in Petrograd. The concerto orchestra smoothly segued from Tchaikovsky to a lovely piece by Rachmaninoff.

Pausing just inside the doorway, Stevie discreetly opened her evening bag to once again check the contents. Keys and lipstick. Compact mirror with miniature digital camera. Tiny transmitter pack disguised as a cigarette case. Cell phone and ballpoint pen-shaped voice recorder.

The name is Bond. Jayne Bond.

She snapped her bag shut and threw her shoulders back, head held high as she began to casually weave her way through the gathering as if she owned the place. She traded smiles and nods with guests as she passed, stopping occasionally to make inane conversation. Then she moved on as quickly as possible, searching for Weston.

"Try the foie gras, Mrs. Madison."

A sandy-haired waiter approached her with a half-empty tray of hors d'oeuvres and some bad news. Jason leaned in close and lowered his voice. "Emelio wanted you to know there's a problem with the transmitter, but don't worry. We'll get it fixed."

"That's just great. Tell him I have a backup in my purse, but it's going to be muffled," she whispered. Aloud she said, "I'll pass on the duck liver, thanks."

The "waiter" nodded before offering the tray among the nearby guests. A moment later, Jason was swallowed by the crowd and Stevie felt a twinge of unease over how quickly she'd lost sight of him. She wished Emelio were here with her and not just in her head. Knowing he was somewhere in the room would have been a comfort.

She circulated some more, her eyes roaming from face to face, listening to snippets of conversation as she walked by. Just then, she spotted Jack Weston on the dance floor with the wife of the Spanish ambassador. All of her doubts vanished in the space of a breath.

She hoped the earrings' transmitter was working again and that the team could hear her. "I've got him. I have the target in sight."

Like a heat-guided missile, Stevie cut a path through the crowd until she reached his side. Pasting a smile on lips suddenly gone cold, she tapped Señora Maravilla de Guzman on the shoulder. The couple stopped dancing and turned inquiring looks her way.

Stevie dipped her head in greeting to Mrs. Guzman before sliding her gaze to Weston. "Jack. How nice to see you again."

His pale eyes conveyed recognition before he plastered a politician's vague but friendly welcome onto his features. "Have we met? I can't believe I'd forget a face as pretty as yours."

She smiled brightly. "Still playing games, huh? Excuse us, señora. I'm cutting in."

After thanking Mrs. Guzman for the dance, he held out his arms to Stevie. She hoped he didn't notice her hesitation before taking his hand and letting him lead her in a waltz.

"So, Jack. You wanted to discuss my retirement fund?"

He sidestepped her question, instead nodding generally at the crowd. "Good turnout tonight. Are you having a nice time?"

"Marvelous." She angled her head and fluttered her lashes at him. "Weren't you going to convince me not to call a press conference?"

Weston finally looked at her, his eyes narrowed in derision. "Where should I direct my answer? I'm sure you want the best possible voice recording."

Stevie glanced down at the bodice of her formfitting dress, secure in the knowledge that the microphone was actually part of her left earring. "You want to frisk me?"

A flash of sexual interest brought warmth to his pale eyes and she felt him relax a little. "I didn't get the money. Your little story is nothing but opportunistic slander and I'm not paying."

"Oh, you're going to pay, Jack. Much more than you realize. You'll lose everything."

Weston swallowed hard and glanced around. "The dance is over, so if you'll excuse me..."

"What if I won't?" Stevie tightened her grip on his sweaty hand. As the orchestra struck up the next piece, she bared her teeth in a predatory smile. "Try to look romantic, Jack. Let's give the folks something to talk about."

She shifted closer, pretending to nuzzle his neck. When he startled and tried to back away, she simply moved in for the kill. She let her voice slide into a cool, condescending tone as she whispered in his ear.

"I think you'll want to see the videotape I have. It's only a copy, of course, but the picture and sound quality are excellent. Guess you didn't realize the Stocktons had hidden security cameras."

Weston made a choking sound and his skin took on an ugly flush before all color drained from his cheeks. She had him dead to rights and he knew it. His eyes darted around the ballroom again to see who might be watching.

''Why don't we step out on the terrace where this conversation won't be overheard?'' There was a quaver in his voice and his attempt at a smile failed miserably.

She took the arm that he gallantly offered in order to keep up the pretense. Her eyes casually scanned the faces in the crowd, trying to catch sight of one of the ''waiters,'' but she couldn't locate anyone from the agency in the sea of bodies.

Where the hell was the rest of the team?

13

EMELIO HUNCHED OVER the radio transmitter set up in the hotel manager's office. Alex sat in one of the guest chairs while Elliott, a sweaty FBI surveillance tech fresh out of Quantico, monitored the recording equipment.

With his elbows on the desk, a headset over his left ear, he listened to the chatter and music from the charity ball. The rest of the team was patched in on the same frequency, but the only voice he wanted to hear, the only voice he cared about, had a sultry New Orleans drawl.

He closed his eyes, imagining Stevie as she talked her way past the registration desk. She looked extraordinarily beautiful tonight, with smoky shadow elongating her beautiful eyes, her short hair curled into golden waves. The white gown she wore skimmed her body like water, shimmering softly as she moved.

Pale pink lipstick emphasized the fullness of her lower lip, turning her normal pout into a lush invitation he hadn't been able to resist. He could still taste the intensity of her kiss. Once they wrapped up this case, he planned to take her away somewhere and discover exactly what she'd written in black-lace letter number nine.

He chuckled under his breath while Stevie talked about somebody named "Og." Her spiel was brash, confident, however he detected an undercurrent of hesitation. Though she worked hard to hide it, her voice had an almost fragile quality that made him wish he could be there beside her.

But he knew how strong she was, both physically and emotionally. Even after all she'd been through, all she'd survived, she hadn't lost her sense of humor or her grace. He also knew how determined she was, how much she needed to have control over her life.

Braga would be the last in a long line of people who'd threatened her independence and identity. The rest of the team was hell-bent on taking Braga down, but Stevie just wanted to make sure she never had to run or be afraid again.

''Of course you're on the guest list. Please enjoy your evening.''

Emelio's shoulders sagged in relief when he heard the registrar's words. He grinned with pride as he softly congratulated her. ''Good work, Jayne. You did it.'' Just then static burst over the headset, followed by intermittent sound and silence.

''Uh, I think maybe we lost a couple of units.''

He scowled over at Elliott since he was stating the obvious, then reached out to flip on the microphone. ''Double O Team, this is Team Leader. Sound check.''

Alex hovered over his shoulder. ''Switch to the other preset channel.''

''Double O Team, can you hear me?''

''Double O Five. Yeah, Leader. I hear you,'' Jason replied. Rick and Dave Heintz checked in, as well, but neither Stevie nor the other three agents answered.

Emelio kept his tone coolly professional, but his

pulse quickened as worry crept along his nerves. "What's the status on 007?"

"Double O Eight, here. I lost track of her."

"Double O Six. I don't see her, either."

Emelio wavered between irritation and concern until Jason spoke quietly over the headset. "Double O Five. I've got her."

What the hell was wrong with her transmitter? He wouldn't be at peace until she was safely back upstairs. "Acknowledged. Let her know there's a problem. Double O Team, maintain visual."

"Double O Eight. Will do, Team Leader, but it's a zoo in here. I've got to fetch another tray of hors d'oeuvres."

Mierda. He dropped his head into his palms. "Get the damned food and get back in the game."

Alex clapped a hand on his shoulder. "Stevie's okay, hombre. She's in a ballroom full of people. Relax."

Frustrated, he turned to offer a rude suggestion that made his partner laugh. Alex propped a hip on the edge of the desk and gave him a sympathetic look. "So, it's that serious, huh?"

Emelio leaned back in the upholstered desk chair and sighed heavily, crossing his arms over his chest. "I didn't even see it coming."

"That's the way it happens, my friend."

His mouth twisted into a humorless smile. "I didn't want it to happen, you know. I thought I could keep it physical. But there's something about her, something special."

"She's the one?"

Emelio pictured her face softly lit by the radiance of dawn, stubbornly determined during an argument, lost in pleasure as they made love. He thought about her passion and her sassiness, her temper and her vulnerability. Stevie was good for him. He needed her. "Yeah, she's the one."

Target in sight... Jack. How nice to...

"She's got him!" He jolted when he heard the snippets of conversation and background noise come through the headphones.

Emelio activated the microphone again. "Double O Team, move in. Now. Don't let that bastard out of sight."

There was no answer. None at all. He flipped levers and turned dials to no avail. All he heard was more static and his own voice cursing in Spanish. Leaning down, he yelled at the radio tech scuttling over his feet beneath the desk.

"Get it in gear, Elliott! I want this thing up and running as of five minutes ago." He shot to his feet, shoving the chair against the wall as he stripped off the headset and tossed it at Alex.

"Where are you going?"

"To the Ball. Cinderella's in trouble."

Alex pitched the headset back to him. "No way, Em. We can't risk it. If Weston sees you now, he'll know for sure he was set up. Let her do her job."

Emelio thought of Stevie, taking on Weston by herself, and cursed some more.

"I WANT THAT VIDEOTAPE, Ms. Madison."

As soon as she left the Grand Ballroom with him, Weston hustled her over to an isolated corner of the veranda. Even in the dark, shrouded by the shadow of cypress and palmetto trees, his pale eyes suddenly glittered with animosity.

"I'm open to negotiation, Jack. What are you offering?"

"How about your continued good health?"

Stevie recoiled, her eyebrows wrinkling in confusion. This was not the same guy she'd walked out the door with. She must have him running scared. "The price of my silence just went up by half. I consider the video a rare collector's item. So now I want to collect seventy-five thousand for it."

He opened his mouth to reply, then snapped it shut. She turned her head to see a couple appear on the stairs below, apparently having been for a stroll through the moonlit hotel gardens. Weston nodded politely, his features once again set in a harmless facade.

As the couple walked by, he stroked his hand over her chest, clumsily fondling her breasts. Anger and humiliation burned her cheeks. Stevie ground the spike heel of her shoe onto his instep. He yelped in pain and loosened his grip.

"Let go of me, asshole."

"Name-calling? Grow up. I want that tape and I want it now." He turned on her, the average-looking, mild-mannered politician gone, and in his place was an adversary who'd just shown his true nature.

Where the hell was her backup team? This wasn't going the way she'd planned. "You're repeating yourself, Jack, and I'm getting bored with the conversation. I'm going back to the ball."

"Sorry you're bored, Stevie. Let me tell you something new." He gripped her upper arm to stop her, hard enough to bruise. "You'd better give me what I want. It would be a shame to destroy that pretty face."

Her temper careened right into *seriously pissed off* and she struck out at him, landing a blow to his shoulder. When he let go of her arm, she got in his face. "You think you can threaten me? Don't make me laugh. You're nothing but Braga's errand boy."

Weston smacked her, hard, across the mouth.

Tears of pain stung her eyes and she gasped. Too stunned to cry out, her mind went numb for a moment, hurling her into the past when another seemingly genteel man had brutalized her without warning. She tasted blood where her bottom teeth cut the inside of her lip.

She looked over at the ballroom doors, concentrating, trying to pick up any sound other than a discouraging silence. The earpiece and transmitter must still be malfunctioning, which meant no one was coming to her rescue.

"Don't underestimate my desperation, Stevie."

She suffered the same jittery anxiety she always felt when her ex-husband was on the verge of exploding. Swallowing hard, she tried to appeal to whatever morality Weston might have left. "You're making a huge mistake, Jack. Do yourself a favor and help me put Braga behind bars. It's the only way—"

His short bark of laughter sounded hollow. "It's too late for that. All I can do now is try to buy myself some time."

Her heart pounded unevenly in her chest. "Jack, listen to me. You know better than anyone how valuable your testimony against Braga would be. As soon as I turn that video over to the Feds, you'll lose any bargaining power you had."

Weston shook his head, a chilling finality clouding

his eyes. "I've already sold my soul. And now it's time to pay the devil his due. You're coming with me."

Raised voices, pealing with laughter, approached from off to the side. People were coming out onto the veranda. This was her chance. Stevie opened her mouth to scream, only to have the sound die stillborn when Weston grabbed her neck, choking her.

"You don't want to do that."

He cut off her air, a reminder of who was in control. Pulling her close, into the embrace of the enemy, he brushed his lips across her ear. "Try to look romantic, Stevie."

It was a sick replay of the scene she'd made inside. She glanced over his shoulder, frantic to make contact with the people milling about in the cool night air. But it was too dark in this corner and their lovers' pose looked too authentic.

Fairy lights danced before her eyes as her lungs burned from lack of oxygen. Weston reached behind him under his tuxedo jacket. When he brought his arm back around, he made sure she saw the gun he was holding. He finally eased the pressure on her windpipe. Stevie gulped in drafts of air while he murmured quiet threats.

"In a minute, I'm going to let you go. Then you and I are going to walk through the garden to another entrance of the hotel." He squeezed her throat again until she nodded her understanding. Then he slipped the gun into his jacket pocket. "Good girl. You do as you're told and you won't get hurt."

Her stomach clenched against a wave of nausea. Her ex-husband Tom had often phrased his words to sound like that, giving her false hope that if she just followed his instructions and catered to his whims, he wouldn't punish her.

The boisterous group returned to the White Orchid Ball, leaving them once again alone on the veranda. Weston gave her a little shove toward the stairs, then moved right behind her, his arm securely around her back. She was so scared. Emelio—

No, she couldn't think about him now. She was on her own, with only her wits and training to rely on.

She pretended to stumble into a ceramic urn filled with geraniums at the bottom of the stairs. When Weston tried to steady her, she jammed her right elbow into his side. He must have suspected she would try something, however. In the next instant she felt the hard point of the gun against her breast.

"The next time you try something, if you make one wrong move, just one, I'll leave you to die among the flowers."

Weston pushed her forward, following closely behind as they entered the garden. Under cover of darkness, Stevie slid one hand into her evening bag and scrambled through the contents. She moved the voice-activated pen to the top and left the bag's clasp open slightly.

The pen would capture whatever happened next on its digital recorder. She only hoped it didn't record her last words.

"So, Ms. Madison. We meet again."

Emelio damn near leaped out of his skin as Braga's supple, resonant voice came over the speaker. Elliott had finally gotten the equipment to work, only for him to have to hear this. Acid churned in his stomach as he quickly flipped the microphone switch and ordered the men to stay quiet.

"Team Leader. I want radio silence."

The hotel manager's office was so still he could hear his heart thudding in his chest. There was a scrabbling sound followed by a loud gasp. Then he heard Stevie, making every effort to come across as brave and in control.

"I wish I could say it was a pleasure, Mr. Braga. You might have picked a meeting room with fresh paint and some furniture."

Braga chuckled humorlessly. "I apologize for the poor accommodations, however you won't be here for long."

"Well, in that case, I'll just be going now."

He made a tutting noise and sighed. "That won't be possible, I'm afraid."

"I don't know anything." Stevie's response had an edge of panic that echoed in the room where she was being held. "Just because I saw you and Weston together—"

"Is reason enough, my dear."

Someone cleared his throat, then Emelio recognized Jack Weston's voice. "She has a videotape of our meeting in Palm Beach last year."

In the ominous silence that followed, he thought he heard something familiar in the background. Emelio leaned over and whispered to Alex. "What is that faint clanging?"

His partner frowned, concentrating. "Metal on metal, something being opened manually, whirring…"

"Freight elevator?"

Before he could be certain, Braga spoke again.

"There is a videotape. How is such a thing possible? You had assured me—"

Jack stammered. *"I didn't know, I swear. There was no way to know they had hidden surveillance."*

"Where is the tape, Ms. Madison?" Braga asked.

"It's safely hidden. You'll get it once I've been paid." Stevie was still trying to maintain the blackmail pretense.

"Mr. Weston, perhaps you can convince her to be more specific?"

"My pleasure."

"Keep your hands off me, Jack..."

There was a scuffle and he heard Stevie cry out. Emelio closed his eyes, sickened by the sound of grunts and blows, flesh smacking flesh. He felt so damn helpless! If only he knew where she was.

"Enough!" Whatever Braga did got immediate results because the fighting stopped. *"Get up, Mr. Weston."*

Emelio opened his eyes and smirked. "That's my girl," he whispered.

"Very impressive, Ms. Madison. Maybe I should offer you a job in my organization."

Jack protested. *"Damn it, it's not my fault—"*

The reply was a blend of sympathy and steel. *"Nothing is ever your fault, Mr. Weston. I trust that you were more cautious this time?"*

"What do you mean? Even if someone saw us leave the party, I made sure they'd think it was for sex."

Braga raised his voice. *"Have you frisked her, you imbecile? Did you make certain she isn't wearing a wire?"*

Jack answered defensively. *"Where would she hide*

one in that dress? I felt her. There's nothing in her cleavage or around her back.''

Impotent rage, hot and murderous, had Emelio clenching his fists. Weston had dared to touch her. He'd put his hands on her and... Then he thought only of Stevie, how much she hated being vulnerable. He couldn't imagine how she'd suffered from that kind of degrading assault. When he growled in frustration, Alex spoke softly behind him. ''We'll get him, hombre. Stay focused.''

''What about her evening bag, Mr. Weston?''

''Oh. I, uh... Give me that!'' Jack demanded. Emelio heard keys jangling, several thuds, the metallic clink of loose change—everything in Stevie's purse hitting the floor. *''See, there's nothing here.''*

''Luckily for you.''

Jack's voice rose in volume. *''Wait. What are you—''*

''Your incompetence has rendered you an unacceptable liability, Mr. Weston.''

''Wait a minute!''

Two distinct coughlike noises, the sound of a gun with a silencer being fired, were followed by Stevie's keening wail. For a second Emilio was too stunned to react. Then cold fear stabbed him through the gut. ''Oh, shit, Alex. We've got to find her. We've got to find her.''

''Where is that videotape?'' Braga's voice lashed out. *''Tell me! Or the next one is for you.''*

''It's in my apartment! It's on the shelf in my apartment.''

Emelio's heart fractured as her ragged whispers carried across the radio waves. *''Oh my God. You killed him. Oh my God.''*

BRAGA DIDN'T BOTHER to keep her from escaping. Instead, he used the brittle silence like a weapon.

He let the smoky metallic scent of gunpowder and the thickly sweet stench of blood beat her into submission. With no more than the sight of that gun still in his hand, the knowledge of the hole a bullet would carve through the back of her skull, Braga kept her in place.

Weston's body lay sprawled on one of the canvas painter's tarps covering the floor. In a moment of shock-induced insanity, Stevie wondered if a coat of white latex would be able to hide the mess on the wall. She turned away, wrapping her arms around her waist.

She'd earned decent scores in her Tactical Firearms course. But nothing could have prepared her for this. It was one thing to test-fire a gun, to put nine bullets into a paper target. It was something else to see a man's head blown into a hundred fragments.

None of her training had taught her how to erase the image of a dead man from her mind. Stevie gave a soft, bitter laugh. Emelio was right. She could take all of the secret-agent classes she wanted, but reality was the harshest of teachers.

Braga walked toward her, tapping the gun against his left thigh. A pleasant half smile added to the attractiveness of his face, the salt-and-pepper hair giving him a distinguished appearance. He seemed perfectly content where he stood, posture militarily correct, studying her through eyes so dark as to appear black.

"You find the situation amusing, Ms. Madison?"

She shifted from one foot to the other on high heels and shaky legs, a chill prancing along her skin. She shouldn't have called attention to herself. "Sometimes you have to look for the humor in life, Mr. Braga."

"Then you will die laughing. How nice for you."

Stevie stared at him, her heart cold and still despite the amiable tone of his voice. He could just as easily have been discussing the weather. No matter what expression his face took on, no matter how smoothly he delivered his words, his eyes still had a reptilian quality.

Braga was handsome, charming, vicious. Just like Tom.

Past terrors and the present danger combined to gnaw away at what little hope she had left. The Smith-Carlyle had four hundred guest rooms, three ballrooms and nine meeting rooms in addition to the offices. With her damn transmitter malfunctioning, she had no way to let the Double O Team know where she was.

"Nothing else to say, my dear? I thought not." Braga angled his head, narrowing his eyes as though measuring her worth. "Sanchez should have to watch your life spill onto cold, hard concrete. But perhaps I will save myself the effort of dragging you to another location. Which would you prefer?"

Neither option was particularly appealing. She stayed quiet, and utterly still, the primitive part of her brain wanting to believe she'd be safe as long as she didn't so much as blink.

"Answer me."

Moving faster than she could react, Braga's fingers tangled in her hair as he raised the gun to eye level. Her heart seized and she held her breath. Stevie stared down the long, black muzzle, afraid of seeing the bullet in its chamber where it waited to end her life.

He yanked her hair, pulling several strands out by the root. "I am waiting for your answer, Ms. Madison. Shall I kill you now, or should I wait?"

"Wait." The words were a hoarse plea forced past the dryness of her throat.

"Say please."

"Wh-What?" She dared to look away from the gun to the stark expression on his face.

His words were soft, yet rich with menace, a reprimand to a disobedient child. "You forgot your manners. You have to say please."

Braga had the voice of an evangelist, or a psychopath, slick and seductive and oh so full of insinuation and threat. She didn't hear him anymore, but instead whispers of the past echoed in her memory. Old voices—her ex-husband, her ex-family—voices she'd locked away in the back of her mind seeped under the door she'd tried so hard to slam on them.

If you'd just be a good girl, a good wife, a good victim…

Her whisper was the smallest of sounds, like a ghost floating over a grave. "Please."

"Please wait, Señor Braga," he prompted, caressing her right temple with the brushed steel of the barrel.

She gasped and squeezed her eyes shut. "Please. Wait."

"As you wish, my dear." Braga abruptly released her hair and stepped back, his voice once again pleasant.

Her eyes popped open in disbelief. She watched him lower the gun and stroll casually across the room, away from her, as if her presence was already forgotten.

"Felipe. *Venga aqui.*"

The door to the meeting room opened and a young Hispanic man responded to Braga's call. *"Sí, jefe?"*

"Go and bring the car around."

Her legs gave way and she slumped to her knees on the industrial-grade carpet. Stevie dropped her chin to her chest and tears spilled onto the hands clenched together in her lap. She should move. She should jump up and run for the door, yanking it open to scream for help.

But, alone and consumed by desolate anguish, she didn't. It wasn't just the fear that paralyzed her. It was the humiliation. It was the shame. She experienced the kind of dread only an abused woman can know. Braga had made her beg for her life and she didn't doubt for a second that he'd make her beg again.

14

EMELIO'S THOUGHTS SWIRLED around his mind as he tried to piece things together. Stevie's life could be measured in a matter of minutes, maybe even seconds, which would pass all too quickly. He drew a deep breath, dispelling the ghosts of mistakes past. He would find her. He had to.

Time was the key. He twisted his wrist and stared at his watch. How long had it been from the time Stevie found Weston to when he heard Braga's voice? No more than fifteen minutes, twenty tops. It wasn't enough time. There was no way Weston could have gotten her out of the hotel, into a car and off Key Biscayne.

"Elliott. Find out if hotel security got anything on the entrance cameras. Move."

Something Stevie had said about paint and furniture triggered his memory. Suddenly words he'd written off as nervous sarcasm became a clear message. He turned to Alex, who was replaying the audio recording, listening for clues.

"Hey, man. When you did a recon of the hotel, didn't you say they were redecorating?"

"Yeah, the small conference rooms on the basement level... Em, that's it! She's got to be in one of those."

Emelio picked up the headset and activated the microphone. ''Double O Team, this is Team Leader. Head for the lowest level of the hotel, but don't be seen.''

''Leader, this is 005. What's happening?'' Jason asked.

''We think we've located 007. Maintain radio silence and wait for further instructions. Team Leader, out.''

Alex rifled through the hotel blueprints. He found the one he wanted and spread it over the desk. ''Okay. We've got a central hallway with meeting rooms on either side. The elevators are in the middle of the south wall—guests to the west, freight on the east. Emergency exits are here and here, doors to the parking garage here.''

Emelio indicated the south wall. ''There are four possible rooms she could be in. But, if you're right about the sound of the freight elevator, that narrows it to these two right here. I want to make sure we're headed in the right direction. Give me your cell phone.''

''What?''

''It has Stevie's number stored in the address book.''

His heart knocked in his chest as he listened to Braga terrorize her. Time was running out. The ringing in his ear echoed over the audio speaker. Emelio muted the volume on the equipment as Braga ordered her to answer the call.

''Stevie Madison speaking.''

Her quiet Southern drawl washed over him. He closed his eyes, searching with his soul, seeking her out in the darkness with messages of reassurance and love.

"I'm coming for you."

"Emelio." There were tears in her voice. It quavered with a combination of misery and hope. "Are you still in Naples?"

He couldn't help a tiny smile. Even with her life on the line, she thought fast and tried to buy him some extra time. Stephanie was an incredible woman. His woman.

"Are you still in the hotel, Jayne?"

"Yes, I'm fine."

Just as he started to speak again, the phone was wrenched from her grasp. The next voice was as warm as winter, confident as only power can be.

"Sanchez. Do you know who this is?"

Stevie's life depended on his ability to paint a picture of surprise. "Braga? What are you doing with her? What the hell is going on?"

"Ms. Madison and I are getting acquainted." Braga paused while he waited for a response. "Don't you want to ask why, Sanchez?"

He said nothing. He would learn more by staying quiet and letting Braga tell him what he already knew.

"*Hijo de puta!* Have you forgotten her so quickly?"

Emelio knew the "her" referred to wasn't Stevie, but he ignored the question, adding fuel to Braga's rage. An angry man was more likely to make errors. That's why his own fury had to wait for release.

"What is it you want?"

Braga inhaled sharply then his voice calmed again. "There is a videotape. I'm sure you know which one I am talking about. Ms. Madison says she has it in her apartment. I have Ms. Madison."

Not for long, you sadistic bastard. "Put her back on the phone. I don't know where it is—"

"Find it! I want the original and every copy."

"I need time, damn it! She ditched me in Naples and I'm on the road headed back to Miami. Let her tell me where it is."

"*No me vengas con tus pendejadas.* You remember how to get to the warehouse in Overtown." That last was a statement, not a question. "This is a simple business transaction. However if something were to go wrong, something unfortunate..."

Memories assaulted him, flooding Emelio's heart with guilt and self-doubt. It was his responsibility to protect Stevie, as it had been to protect Lina. He answered the only way he could, a single affirmative forced past the tightness in his throat.

"We understand each other, then. You have ninety minutes, Sanchez. Believe me, you do not want to be late." The cell phone disconnected.

Emelio closed his eyes and inhaled deeply, dragging air into suddenly constricted lungs. Fear, stark and vivid, punctured his chest when he couldn't stop the images of what Braga might do to the woman he loved. He opened his eyes and turned to his partner.

Alex pulled off the headphones he'd been using to follow the conversation. His best friend looked at him with a steady green gaze. "Braga won't settle for the video. Have you thought about that?"

"Only every fifteen seconds or so." He scrubbed a hand over his face.

"With a single exception, you've always played by the rules, hombre. Do you want me to take this one?" His expression said there was no conceit or disrespect in his offer, that it wouldn't change anything between them.

But Emelio shook his head. "I'm playing winner takes all."

Alex nodded and grabbed a roll of electrical tape out of Elliott's equipment bag. "I've got an idea. Strip off your jacket and open your shirt."

"What the hell is that for?" Emelio nodded at the roll of tape as he tugged off his suit coat.

"You're going to need an ace in the hole. I saw that *Die Hard* movie on cable last night so—"

"So you're going to turn me into an action hero. That means I need a couple minutes lead on the rest of the team. I can't take a chance on anyone getting overzealous."

Emelio pulled his Ruger from its shoulder holster. Braga might decide to kill her now, instead of waiting for him. He thought about Stevie and her James Bond movies, wondering if he had it in him to be the kind of hero she needed right now.

Moments later, the cuffs of his shirt were rolled to his elbows, the front unbuttoned to the middle of his chest. On his upper back, just below the collar, Alex had used the electrical tape to secure the Beretta at the base of his neck. His partner flicked the microphone for the speaker.

"Double O Team, take the fire stairs, not the elevators. Set up at either end of the main corridor, then sit tight."

Jason acknowledged the order. "Double O Five, roger that. We'll be in position in less than ten."

That meant he had less than five. Alex glanced at him and elevated his thumb before extending his index finger, their signal for "good to go, move your ass.'' Emelio grabbed the cell phone and ran through the hotel lobby, ignoring the startled looks of the guests he brushed aside. He leaped down the curved staircase to the lower level then paused.

Watching, listening and praying.

It all came down to trust. Lina had trusted him and he'd lied to her. He had trusted her and she'd betrayed him. He'd trusted Stevie and she had walked into a trap. The only person left to trust was himself.

Wild, restless anger burned away his uncertainty, leaving behind the heat he needed to go after Braga. At the end of the night, one of them would walk away. The other would be carried.

But no matter what, Stevie would live.

EMELIO WAS COMING.

Stevie assumed her transmitter must be working after all, though she still heard nothing but static through the earpiece. He'd figured out how to find her, but his life would be over as soon as he came through the door. Braga might want the videotape but, judging by his comments, he wanted revenge even more.

She righted herself from where he'd pushed her to the floor when he took her cell phone. Listening to his end of the conversation, it was obvious he had planned to kill Emelio at the warehouse all along. If there was anything in her power to prevent it, she had to act. Now.

Emelio was the only person in her life who'd ever truly accepted her for who she was. He had proven earlier tonight that he trusted her, that he believed in her. In loving Emelio, she found the strength she needed for her training to finally override her fear.

She had to fight for him, for their love and for her own self-respect.

"Carlos. I want to talk to you." Braga tossed the phone on top of the evening bag beside her. Without a backward glance, he stepped out of the room, closing the door behind him.

Stevie seized the moment. Scrambling on her hands and knees, she swallowed her revulsion at having to get close to Weston's body. Quickly reaching into his tuxedo jacket, she pulled the gun from his pocket.

Hoo yah. A Walther PPK/S .380 caliber blued steel double action combat pistol. Jayne Bond's weapon of choice.

After a swift glance at the door, she tried to decide where to put it. She looked at the contents of her purse scattered on the carpet, then dismissed the idea of hiding the gun in there. It would be too obvious and too difficult to access later.

Stevie rushed back to her place on the floor, plunged her hand through the split in her dress and shoved the pistol into her left stocking garter. It felt cold and hard against her thigh and it was positioned awkwardly. However, she'd just have to deal with the discomfort and pray it didn't slide down her leg when she stood up.

As the door opened, she dropped her head and concentrated on looking despondent. It wasn't hard with her heart pounding against her ribs and a light sweat breaking out on her skin.

Braga came back into the room with his two thugs. He waved a hand at Weston's body. "Wrap that garbage in the drop cloths and dispose of it. Help him, Felipe."

Stevie kept her head down. She couldn't let on that

anything about the situation had changed. Braga had to believe she was still under his control. But she wasn't, and she never would be again.

THE LOWER LEVEL OF THE HOTEL was dark; only minimal lighting pierced the quiet shadows along the main corridor. In the stillness, Emelio's pulse ticked away the minutes left in Stevie's life.

At the bottom of the stairs, he ducked into an empty meeting room to hide. Where was she? Which room? He wanted to kick in every door until he found her, but knew that losing the element of surprise would get her killed.

From down the hall, the sounds of heavy, arrhythmic footfalls were punctuated by soft grunts. He took a chance and peered around the doorway to see two men come into sight, balancing a long canvas painter's drop cloth between them.

Part of him mourned Weston's death. Jack was an avaricious traitor who had betrayed everything Emelio believed about honor and justice. But he should have rotted in a federal prison, not in a shallow grave by the side of a back road.

The two men came near enough for Emelio to make out their words. "It will have to wait, Felipe."

"But *el jefe* said to get rid of—"

"There are too many people around, *estupido*. Weston has to stay in the trunk."

Emelio flattened himself against the wall until he heard them go past. Peering through the crack of the door frame, he watched Jason and Heintz step out of the dark alcove near the parking-garage entrance. Guns at the ready, they moved as one to stop Carlos and Felipe before they could raise an alarm.

Once the SOD had the two henchmen safely in custody, Emelio hurried down the corridor in the direction they had come. Stevie was in one of the rooms next to the freight elevator, he was sure of it. But which one? He pressed the redial button on Alex's cell phone, letting it ring only once.

HOW LONG DID IT TAKE to get rid of a body? Stevie had no idea, but figured it wouldn't take long enough. She turned her head away and tried to block out the sounds of the late Jack Weston being lifted and carried out of the room. She had to figure out what to do next.

She tried to remember the lessons from her Hostage Survival class. Stevie drew a shallow breath, determined to make Braga see her as a person and not another liability. "So, what's next? I have friends, family. People will be looking for me."

"Let them look." Braga pulled back the sleeve of his tuxedo and looked at his watch. "As soon as Carlos and Felipe return, we will leave for the warehouse. I do hope Sanchez is able to find that videotape."

"Why are we going to Overtown?"

Braga's features darkened and his mouth twisted into a frown. He answered almost to himself, muttering, "It seemed appropriate to return to the scene of Sanchez's crime."

"I don't know what you're talking about. What did he—"

"Enough questions, Ms. Madison. I have no intention of explaining myself to you."

"No small talk? No chitchat?" Stevie shook her head. "No one takes the time to do a really sinister interrogation anymore."

Braga's smile was arctic. "There will be time enough to find out what little you know. You're quite clever, for a woman. But I doubt that Sanchez would trust you with any real knowledge of my business."

His assumption was too close to the argument she'd had with Emelio that morning. But Stevie resented the hell out of being dismissed and felt the welcome spark of temper. "You can't be sure of that. Maybe I've already turned everything I have over to the authorities."

"I hope not. For your sake." Braga reached down to pat her cheek. "However, I do not anticipate any problems escaping prosecution, just as I have in the past."

"Your arrogance will be your downfall. How do you know Weston wasn't playing both sides, too? You were a fool to trust a rat like him."

He frowned and his eyes flashed like black diamonds, though she wasn't sure whether it was in reaction to being called a fool or to the idea of Weston double-crossing him. "It does not matter. With both of you dead, there will be no one to corroborate any accusations."

"You won't get away with—"

"Please, my dear, do not resort to clichés."

Stevie blinked while he laughed at her. So much for getting a confession on her pen recorder. She was just about to ask another question when her cell phone rang. It chimed once and then lay quiet. Was that some kind of signal?

EMELIO STOOD OUTSIDE the door to the right of the elevators, heart racing. Adrenaline rushed through his bloodstream. He shrugged his shoulders to make sure the shirt was loose enough to reach beneath it. Then he lifted his fist to knock.

Just then, Braga's voice came from the inside. "*Mierda!* Where are those two?"

Emelio rapped his knuckles against the wood. A startled, electric silence greeted the sound. He knocked again, louder. Finally Braga replied, "Carlos, you imbecile, get in here."

He raised one arm behind his head then turned the knob just enough to open the door. Behind him, he heard Jason whisper, "What the hell are you doing?"

Emelio ignored him, except to give a gesture ordering the team to stay back for now. He nudged the door wider with his foot and stepped into the room, raising his other arm and lacing the fingers together. His eyes scanned the thirty-by-thirty-foot meeting space, assessing the situation.

His gaze settled on Stephanie. She was on her knees in the center of the room, head bowed over her hands. Even at a distance, he could see that her pale cheeks were wet with tears, her features set in a forlorn expression.

An almost uncontrollable rage choked him, burning away all other emotion. It infuriated him to see her subjugated this way, bereft of her usual vitality and sass. His fingers itched to reach for his gun. Damned if he would let Braga have the satisfaction of breaking her spirit.

"Sanchez!"

At the startled exclamation, Emelio turned his attention to his nemesis. Braga's face registered shock and recognition before yielding to anger. His eyes narrowed dangerously as he realized he'd been caught in his own trap.

Braga brought the Glock 29 up and pointed it at Stevie's head. His resonant voice oozed frigid sarcasm. "You must be one hell of a fast driver, Sanchez. You've arrived just in time to watch her die."

Emelio's heart stopped, trapping his breath in his throat. He risked breaking eye contact long enough to glance at Stevie. She looked scared, but in her eyes he saw hope, and then she had the audacity to wink at him.

It threw him off for a second but he refocused. He took several steps farther into the room, talking fast to keep Braga from pulling the trigger. "Don't do it. There's only one way out of this room and the hallway is filled with cops. It's over."

Braga's eyes darted toward the door, but his aim never wavered. His gun was still trained on Stevie.

"It's over. Carlos and Felipe are under arrest. We have Weston's death on audiotape and Stevie is an eyewitness." He walked closer still, moving to his left to hold Braga's attention. "We've got you for jury tampering, conspiracy, kidnapping and murder. No way are you going to skate on the charges this time."

Braga stared him down. "In that case, I have nothing more to lose. I may go to jail but I will have my revenge."

Out of the corner of his eye, Emelio saw Stevie reach under her dress and draw out a pistol. *Dios mio,* what a woman. She was constantly surprising him. He struggled not to betray her with his reaction.

"Let Stevie go. She has nothing to do with this. Let her go and take me in her place."

Braga's laugh was devoid of humor. "She has everything to do with this. You are lovers. You care for her. I want you to have to watch as she dies, just as I had to watch Carolína."

"Lina never would have been in that warehouse if you hadn't involved her in your criminal activity. You gave her that travel business, with everything in her name, so that she would take the fall if anything went wrong."

"No! I protected her. Nothing would have happened to her if you had not interfered. It was you who made her betray her family. You are responsible for her death!"

Emelio flinched under the weight of the accusation. "God knows, I never meant for her to get hurt. I didn't directly involve her in the investigation until the very end."

Braga scoffed contemptuously. "She was part of it long before you knew. You thought you were so smart, Sanchez. But I was one step ahead of you all the time."

"What are you talking about?"

"My cousin came to me. She confessed." Braga's smile was terrible to see. "Any information she gave you after that was only what I wanted you to know."

Emelio's voice was a hoarse whisper. "I don't believe it."

"Face it, Sanchez. A young woman's lust may have been easy for you to manipulate, but her guilt was even easier. She owed me her loyalty and she paid for her betrayal."

He stared at Braga, unnerved, as the truth hit him full force. "Overtown was an ambush. You cold-blooded son of a bitch. You didn't just trap Lina in the middle of your deal. You set her up for execution."

A kind of madness gleamed in Braga's eyes, his expression one of barely leashed fury. "She was pure until she began a relationship with you! You took a sweet young girl and corrupted her for your own pleasure. Once you had her, she was forever tainted. She was never the same!"

Emelio's mouth twisted into a sad smile as the weight of failure lifted from his shoulders. He'd thought that Lina offered to help him out of love, but she had only been working for her cousin. Perhaps he'd broken the rules and lost sight of his responsibility. Maybe Braga had used and manipulated her. But, in the end, the truth was that Lina made her own choices.

For the past two years he'd been seeking forgiveness, trying to regain his lost honor. He realized now that the only person he needed to forgive him was himself.

"Lina knew what she was doing."

"She did not! Carolína was my angel, she was everything good and pure. You ruined her!"

Emelio noticed Stevie shift her position on the floor and glanced over at her. She lifted her hand just enough for him to see the Walther, then nodded once. Whatever happened next, she was ready. He had to be, also.

He bent his right elbow toward the Ruger, then made certain Braga's anger and attention stayed focused on him. "You were jealous, is that it? You planned to have her to yourself. But then she chose me. You lied to and controlled and exploited Lina because she slept with me."

"*Cálle te!* Shut your mouth."

"She gave herself to me, not to you. That's it, isn't it? You wanted her in your bed and she refused you."

Braga's face turned purple with rage as he swung the Glock 29 in his direction. "May you rot in hell, Sanchez."

EMELIO WAS GOING TO DIE unless she saved him.

Once upon a lifetime ago, Stevie had begged, she'd pleaded until she had no self-esteem left, no confidence and no faith. Just as she had pleaded with Braga a short while ago. She'd felt so helpless, so lost and alone that she didn't believe she could save herself.

But now it was Emelio in danger, Emelio who needed to be saved. This time she wasn't going to cower or crawl. This time she'd stand up to her abuser—it was the only way to truly be free. And, in doing so, she could regain the control she'd finally achieved over her life. She couldn't go down without a fight, not when she had the power to save the man she loved.

The Walther weighed more heavily on her mind than in her hand. She'd never be able to callously murder someone, not after seeing Weston meet such a violent end. But she could sure as hell pop a cap into Braga's left shoulder.

Stevie levered up on her knees and brought her pistol up, flexing her thighs for balance. She pulled the bolt back in order to load the first round. The harsh metallic click of the bullet sliding into the chamber echoed loudly in the empty room.

At the sound, Braga swung his head in her direction, stunned disbelief evident on his face. Bracing her wrist, Stevie narrowed her eyes and sighted down the barrel. Looking right into Braga's cold black eyes, she squeezed the trigger.

Emelio arced his right arm over his shoulder, a gun appearing suddenly in his hand. He fired at the same time she did, the double blast deafening in the small room. Braga cried out, dropping his gun and falling backward under the impact of the two bullets striking his upper body.

"Shots fired! Move! Move! Who's hit?" The Double O Team rushed through the door, quickly filling the meeting room with more guns and a lot of testosterone.

Emelio kicked Braga's gun out of reach then he offered his hand, pulling Stevie to her feet. She continued to stare at Braga as he writhed on the floor, bleeding and in pain. She tossed her own gun aside, sickened by what she'd had to do.

IT WAS FINALLY OVER.

No more running. No more hiding. No more fear.

As the Double O Team waited for an ambulance to take Braga away, Stevie squeezed Emelio's hand and turned to look at him. Her gaze drank in the sight of his devastatingly handsome face. His golden skin was still pale and stretched tightly over his regal cheekbones. Everything he felt for her showed in the depths of his hazel eyes.

God, how she loved him. She loved him for his sensitivity and his dedication to his job, his loyalty and even his protectiveness. She loved his ever-present sex appeal and his creative spirit. Through the power of love, she had survived and she had triumphed. She had a future in which she'd never be a victim again, a future she hoped to share with the man who'd made it possible.

The aftermath of an adrenaline high slammed into her like a freight train. First came relief and then a weariness like she'd never known before. Then came the tears. Stevie gladly collapsed into the safety of Emelio's embrace, sobbing as he rocked her in his strong arms.

"*Tranquila, mi querida. Tranquila.*" She felt his lips brush her temples as he whispered into her hair. The words were in Spanish, but she understood the soothing comfort. A few moments later, Stevie stepped back and wiped her eyes, while Alex grinned at her and Jason made kissy noises.

Warm color flooded her cheeks. "Shut up, you guys."

Emelio offered her one of his rare smiles. "Get used to it, Stephanie. They'll have to."

"What? This from the guy who was worried about how it would look back at the office?"

"It'll look like this."

He gathered her back into his arms and captured her lips in a kiss that set her hair on fire. It was hot and sweet and full of promise. Stevie wound her arms behind his neck, pulling him closer as desire sang through her blood.

The sound of applause had her stepping back, flustered. "Wow. That was Bond worthy."

"You earned it, Jayne."

"That reminds me. Nice trick with the gun behind your back." Stevie cocked her head to one side. "Maybe next time, though, you could put it somewhere more convenient so I don't have to save your ass."

Emelio crossed his arms over his chest, one eyebrow arched in amused protest. "What are you talking about? You couldn't have saved me—I got off the first shot."

She scoffed. "You're dreaming. I shot first."

"No way, lady. You were still practicing your regulation combat stance when I took Braga out."

"Oh, please. I had him—"

"Yes, you did, Stephanie." Emelio's gaze echoed the soft, enchanting tone of his voice. "I'm so damn proud of you."

Her heart swelled, choking her with emotion. Tears shimmered in her eyes, threatening to set off another torrent of sobs. Her fingers trembled in his grasp and her voice broke. "You have no idea what it means to hear you say that. I've waited my whole life to hear someone say those words."

"I only say it because it's true. You're an incredible woman, Stephanie. Strong, intelligent, passionate." He reached out to cup her face in his palm. "All joking aside, you did save my life. In more ways than one."

Stevie returned his quiet smile. "We saved each other."

15

ONCE THE PARAMEDICS ARRIVED, there wasn't enough space in the meeting room for Emelio, Alex and six other agents, Braga's animosity, Oscar Solis's egotistical gloating and Stevie, too. So when Emelio suggested she go upstairs to the hotel manager's office and wait for him, she gratefully fled the scene.

She sat down in the upholstered chair and braced her elbows on the desktop. She sighed, resting her forehead in her palms. Fatigue settled onto her shoulders, weighing her down. Stevie leaned back in the chair and closed her eyes.

Braga smiled menacingly and then his features melted into Tom's. She screamed, but the sound was muffled as she shot the men who'd threatened her.

"It's over, Stephanie."

She must have dozed off because she startled when Emelio gently shook her arm. She dragged in a shuddering breath and sat up. He crouched down beside the chair and wiped the dampness from her cheeks with the pad of his thumb.

"It's all right now. You're safe."

Her throat felt tight with the residue of the horrific images in her mind. "I was dreaming."

Emelio soothed her, his voice calm and understanding. "I know, *querida.* And I won't lie to you—there will be other dreams. But in time, it won't be as bad."

For the rest of her days, Stevie knew she would remember what it was like to point a gun at another living soul and pull the trigger because she had no choice. She only hoped he was right about the healing power of time. She swiped the last tears away and offered Emelio a smile of thanks.

He looked as tired as she felt. The shadows in his expression reminded her that he'd been awake and under stress for almost two days. However, the gleam in his eyes suggested that his voice was rough with something other than weariness.

"Why don't we leave the debriefings and the paperwork until tomorrow—Alex and Solis can handle things. I'll take you up to your room."

She pushed back from the desk and took his hand. Arousal warmed her skin and sped desire through her veins, making her forget her fatigue. "Is this the part of the movie where we indulge in life-affirming sex after narrowly escaping death and triumphing over the bad guys?"

"Yes, I believe it is."

His mouth curved into a sensual smile. He stroked his thumb across her knuckles, sending a shiver of awareness along her nerves. The breath hitched in her throat as a reckless yearning coiled inside her. In that instant, she wanted nothing more than to be naked in his arms. She wanted to hold him close and make love until she forgot everything that happened tonight.

"Did you have anything particular in mind, chér?"

"Black-lace letter number nine."

He lifted their joined hands to press a kiss onto her wrist. Then he grabbed his suit jacket from the back of one of the guest chairs and led her from the room. Upstairs in her suite, a single lamp cast a golden glow over the green-and-white walls. A cool breeze from the open balcony doors filled the room with the fragrant scent of jasmine.

Emelio gathered her into his arms, holding her tightly in his embrace. She could feel his heart beating in time with her own, confirming that they were still alive, making her more aware of what they'd almost lost.

He must have sensed her melancholy because he angled his face to kiss her forehead, her temples and cheeks, before brushing his lips over her mouth. She wrapped her arms more tightly about his waist and parted her lips for his tongue.

She opened to him, to the tenderness of his slow, healing kiss. Heat, warm and penetrating, increased the need arcing between them until the kiss became eager and urgent. Pausing to catch her breath, Stevie tipped her head back and looked into his amber-green eyes.

There she saw desire in their smoldering depths and so much more. So much more. She lifted her hand to caress the side of his face. Something primitive and humbling and powerful connected them. She felt it as surely as his pulse beneath her fingertips. Then she sensed a change in his attitude and saw the gleam of amusement in his gaze.

"Now that we're finally alone, Lacy Sweetbottom, I—"

Stevie burst into surprised laughter.

"What? That's a great name for a Bond girl." He pretended to ignore her interruption. "As I was saying, Lacy, I think it's safe now. You can reveal the contents of the secret document I've been carrying."

Stevie cocked her head to one side, as though considering it. "I don't know. This information is ultra top secret. I'm not certain you have the right security clearance."

Sliding one hand along the curve of her backside, he cupped her sweet bottom and held her against his burgeoning erection. "Are you sure this isn't all I need, 007?"

"It's definitely what I need." Stevie wiggled her eyebrows suggestively, feeling some of her old sass return. "Do you know what the Double O prefix means?"

"No. Why don't you tell me."

"In my case it means I have a license to thrill, darling." She rubbed the hardened peaks of her breasts across his chest. A wonderful pressure tingled in her belly and she shivered in anticipation.

With a wicked grin, he pulled the small envelope from the breast pocket before tossing his jacket onto the wing chair.

When he handed the note to her, she shied away, confused.

"You're supposed to read it out loud, remember?"

Her heart gave a little leap as a delicious ache settled between her thighs. Only a few days ago, the idea of revealing her fantasy this way had embarrassed her. Now, though, she knew without a doubt how safe she was with him and reveled in the seductive delight of his challenge.

Stevie took the envelope and slit it open with her thumb. Emilio perched on the arm of the sofa and waited, the eager light in his hooded eyes adding to the sensual beauty of his face. She unfolded the pearl-gray note card, pitching her voice low and sultry as she began to read.

"In my fantasy, you come to me in darkness, wearing only moonlight and a smile. No words need to be spoken, because you already know my every desire. Each beat of my heart whispers your name as your hands fulfill the secret longings of my body. I want to lose myself in you, to forget everything except the exquisite pleasure of your touch. Come to me, and I'll be yours, in black lace."

Stevie looked up from the letter to gauge Emelio's reaction. At the sight of the heat flaring in his eyes, lust spread like wildfire through her body. A ripple of excitement sang along her nerves and she ached for his touch.

He cleared his throat but the gruffness remained when he teased her. "You were supposed to read it naked."

The slow, insistent throb became a deep pulsating need. She tilted her head, coyly watching him from beneath her lashes as she arched her back and reached around for the zipper. The thin straps of her dress fell from her shoulders and the bodice slipped down her outthrust breasts. When she shrugged, the white satin gown flowed from her body to pool at her feet.

"For your eyes only, chér."

"I'm going to use more than just my eyes."

Emelio felt gravity double in the pit of his stomach as he stood up and prowled toward her in a single movement. She stepped out of the puddle of fabric to stand proudly before him, sexy as hell in nothing but her white-lace panties, thigh-high silk stockings and stiletto heels.

Her body was incredibly beautiful; both sculpted and curvy, toned and soft. Her eyes sparkled like sun rays on the water and her smile made him believe that anything was possible. He couldn't take his eyes off of her. Stevie looked strong and feminine and sensual and alive.

His throat constricted. He could have lost her tonight. Just when they'd found each other and discovered something special, he might have lost her. He knew in his heart that if that had happened, a part of him would have died with her.

Overwhelmed by the intensity of his feelings, he reached for her. She draped her arms behind his neck while his hands skimmed down her bare back. Their lips met and mated as she rocked her hips against his pelvis. She kissed him hungrily, her tongue tracing circles inside of his mouth while her hands slid down to unbutton his shirt.

Then her fingers stole beneath the material to brush his skin in a long, gliding caress. He shivered, his body ever sensitive to her touch. When she pushed the shirt off of his shoulders, the feel of her bare breasts was like warm silk against his chest.

He broke the kiss only long enough to remove his shirt completely. She reached down to unzip his trousers and ease her fingers inside his briefs. Stevie wrapped her fingers around the base of his penis, grasping him firmly in slow up and down strokes. His breath caught as his shaft lengthened and pulsated against her palm.

"Aah, don't do that or this will be the shortest mission of your career."

"Then let's continue this...debriefing in the other room." She turned and walked toward the ornate French doors. Her hips swayed seductively, inviting him to follow her.

At the foot of the bed, Emelio swept a hand over her hair and along her cheeks before cupping the nape of her neck. He sought her lips again more slowly, more tenderly, but with no less passion. They parted for a moment to remove the last of their clothing, then Stevie turned to climb onto the bed.

Light from the full moon filtered through the billowing curtains, illuminating her features and yet keeping her enticingly in shadow as she lifted her arms toward him. He joined her, easing her back onto the smooth linen sheets before covering her body with his own. They lay together, as close as possible without becoming one.

He wanted her. Not only in his bed, but in his heart. Not just for tonight, but every night for the rest of their lives.

Emelio indulged himself in the pleasure of touching her. His hands skimmed over her flawless skin, caressing the toned and sleek muscle, rediscovering the places that were susceptible to certain kinds of fondling. His mouth followed the path his hands had set and she quivered in response to his attentions.

Stevie didn't utter a word as she stirred restlessly beneath him, rocking her hips in subtle encouragement. Her body told him in the language as old as time how much she wanted him. Heat, slow and molten, spread through him as he breathed in the scent of her desire.

Emelio trailed a line of kisses along her throat and over her chest. He slid lower on the bed until her full breasts were accessible for his pleasure. Her hands sought his back, caressing his skin and massaging the muscle below the surface, as he rained kisses onto the soft orbs.

Taking one hard, straining nipple into his mouth, he suckled it to a sensitive peak. His tongue drew lazy swirls around the crest before turning his head to give its mate the same consideration. When his teeth gently scraped her ultraresponsive flesh, she squealed in unabashed delight.

Then he shifted his weight to free his right arm. Emelio reached among the silken curls between her thighs to find her soft feminine folds. Stevie moaned softly and clutched at his shoulder while he rubbed her swollen clitoris in languid circles. She arched her hips against his hand as he slid his fingers in and out of her damp passage.

After making sure they were protected, he moved over her, his body humming with need as he claimed her mouth. She nibbled his bottom lip before thrusting her tongue inside to taste and tease and tantalize. Stevie spread her thighs, draping her calves over his, urging him to claim her completely.

She pressed her mouth to his throat, her hands gripping the hard muscles of his back, while he pushed into her wet passage, inch by inch, drawing out the moment of joining. Incredible emotion and fierce desire combined to intensify the sensation, but he struggled for control.

Her heat enveloped the full length of him before he drew back a little at a time. He built the tension and anticipation, heightening the pleasure while prolonging the climax. Stevie wiggled and strained beneath him, urging him on.

He slipped his palms under her hips, pulling her closer still. The need to be part of her drove him deeper, rocking him to the core. Unable to hold back any longer, he began thrusting heavily and she lifted her body to meet him. He felt the change inside her, felt her tighten around him. He cried out his release as she moaned his name.

Stevie's breath fanned his ear as they held each other. Waiting for his pulse rate to slow, her body still joined with his, Emelio felt a sense of belonging, of union. Each breath seemed to bring them closer together, emotionally as well as physically. There were things that didn't have to be said in order to be known. But he wanted— No, he needed to say the words just the same.

He closed his eyes, suddenly anxious and uncertain. He thought he knew how she felt. What if he was wrong? Stevie had survived one dangerous relationship and the past week had proved that this was another. Considering how she'd reacted to the idea of marriage and children, he was taking a huge risk assuming she wanted the same things he did.

But tonight had shown him that he had to seize the moment. He thought about his life over the recent years, then pictured his future without Stevie by his side. He didn't want to waste another second. She was worth any risk. He inhaled deeply, gathering his courage, and tried to calm his racing heart.

"I love you, Emelio."

His eyes popped open and the breath escaped his lungs in a whoosh. Raising his weight onto his elbows so he could look at her, he let out an involuntary chuckle. There was that control issue again. She couldn't even let him declare his feelings first.

Stevie's stomach lurched and embarrassment flamed onto her cheeks. The heaviness in her chest had nothing to do with Emelio lying on her. She regarded him through a narrowed gaze and forced a joking tone into her voice. "Oh, great. Tell a guy you love him and what does he do? He laughs in your—"

Emelio sealed her lips with his own, effectively stopping her words. His kiss was gentle and sweet and reassuring. Even in the darkness, she could see the emotion in his eyes.

"I love you, too, Stephanie. I thought I knew what love was before, but I was wrong."

"I've been wrong before, too. All of a sudden I feel scared, vulnerable. In the past, everyone I've loved, everyone who was supposed to love me, has hurt me terribly."

He put one arm around her waist and rolled onto his back, enfolding her in his embrace. "I've sworn time and again to protect you. With that comes my promise to honor, cherish and respect you. No one will ever hurt you again, especially not me."

She laid her head on his chest and listened to his heart beating beneath her ear. She wanted to savor the intimacy, the precious connection that bound them together, and have it drive away the uncertainty. "It's been a different kind of hurt. I could never live up to what people expected of me. I couldn't be who they wanted."

"You don't have to be a good girl. You don't have to be a Bond girl. You only need to be yourself for me to love you."

Her anxiety subsided, quieting her erratic pulse. He was saying everything she could want to hear, but she had to be sure. "You told me once that when time gets compressed and emotions run high, what normally take months to develop can happen in a matter of hours. I guess I'm wondering whether a relationship begun in crisis can last."

Emelio held her face in his strong but gentle hand and tilted her chin until she looked at him. He held her gaze, his melodic voice hoarse with feeling, and she saw the promise in his heart. "This is real, Stephanie. This is true. And this is forever."

She felt the last of the darkness inside her shatter, allowing the radiance of his love to fill her heart. At last, she'd found her soul mate, a man she could belong to without ever being a possession. She could be herself. She could lose control. She could love him.

"GET IT IN GEAR, STEPHANIE. We're going to be late for dinner. My mother is making *arroz con pollo* just for you."

"I'm going to weigh three hundred pounds if she keeps feeding me like this."

Emelio chuckled over Stevie's half-muttered comment from the bathroom as he pulled a raspberry-colored polo shirt over his head. She was nowhere near three hundred pounds, but her athletic figure had softened and expanded over the past four months. He smiled to himself. The one time they'd forgotten to use a condom…

"I'm heading downstairs, *querida.*"

"I'll be down as soon as I manage to stretch these pants over my belly."

In the living room of their house in Coral Gables, Emelio made sure everything was ready for later tonight. Satin sheet laid out on the carpet. New sable paint brushes. Caramel ice-cream topping. Hot fudge sauce. Vanilla body frosting. He chose a note card from the box of stationery on the end table and began writing a black-lace letter.

In my fantasy, you'll wear nothing except a pair of panties. I'll lay you down in candlelight, the love in my eyes reflecting the soft glow on your bare skin. I'll take my time, touching and tasting you, enjoying the gasp of my name on your lips. Then, on the canvas of your body, I'll paint my love and you'll be mine, in black lace.

Emelio tucked the note in the pocket of his sport jacket, planning to hand it to Stevie in the car. Then he sat down on the couch to wait for her. He leaned his elbow on the chair arm, resting his chin in his palm, and gazed up at the painting above the credenza. The abstract sunrise he created of Stevie in Naples was the best work he'd done.

The painting represented their discovery of joy and trust, laughter and passion. It symbolized a new beginning for both of them. He heard her enter the room behind him and turned his head to look at her. Stevie was radiant, blossoming in the warmth of their love and her impending motherhood. She reached for him and he glanced down at their joined hands as he stood up.

On her left finger was a three-stone ring that bore the inscription, Diamonds Are Forever. He wore a matching gold band that read, From Stevie With Love. In keeping with her love of all things Bond, he'd flown her to Jamaica to propose at the real Golden Eye estate.

"Okay, chér, let's get this marital madness over with."

During the past four months, his parents, aunts, uncles and cousins had all welcomed her into their loud and affectionate embrace and shown her the true meaning of family. Stevie claimed that the "three *cariñas,*" as she referred to his sisters, were driving her crazy with all of the wedding plans. But there was no denying the gleam of happiness in her eyes.

Emelio gazed at his inspiration, his friend, his future wife, and smiled.